MW01138983

COPYRIGHT

FIRST EDITION

Library of Congress Cataloguing-in-Publication Data has been applied for.

The Passenger

A Surviving the Dead Novel

By
James N. Cook and Joshua Guess

Also by James N. Cook:

Surviving the Dead Series:

No Easy Hope

This Shattered Land

Warrior Within

Also by Joshua Guess:

Victim Zero

Beautiful

Living With the Dead Series:

With Spring Comes the Fall

The Bitter Seasons

The Hungry Land

The Wild Country

This New Disease

American Recovery

Authors' note:

Please Read Before Purchase!

If this is your first visit to the harrowing world of the Surviving the Dead series, feel free to disregard this authors' note entirely. (And yes, I meant for authors' to be plural. There are two of us this time around.) If you are a longtime fan of the series, however, you really need to read this.

For my stalwart friends revisiting this world after several months' absence, I would like to set a few expectations up front.

First of all, this is not Surviving the Dead Volume Four. Eric and Gabriel are not featured in this novel. However, you may remember the main character, and a few others, from my first novel *No Easy Hope*. This is a standalone novel set in the Surviving the Dead universe. This book is not crucial to the overall Surviving the Dead storyline—meaning you can skip it and still follow the series just fine—but you will be missing out if you do.

Second, this novel is written differently than the first three. All my other work is written in the first person, whereas this novel is, for the most part, written in third person. A significant portion is written in first person, but I did not write those sections. My good friend and co-author Joshua Guess did. All my contributions to this novel are, as previously stated, third person.

Why the switch, you ask?

There are several reasons. I wanted to make it clear to you, awesome reader, that this novel is different from the other three. Writing in first person kind of limits your options as a writer, while third person—with its omniscient perspective—provides a great deal more flexibility. You can add plot elements and provide explanations that would be cumbersome in first person. Third person also contributes significantly to brevity, making the writing flow much faster. Mostly, though, I just wanted to try it. I've been writing in first person for so long, I felt like I was starting to stagnate. I think it is important for me to push my limits and try new things as a writer, and to develop new skills.

How did I do? Personally, I think I did okay for a first attempt. I guess I'll have to defer to your judgment on that.

Which is not to say that Joshua didn't write any third person sections. He did. (He is equally good at either perspective, the cocky bastard.) But I'll leave it up to you to figure out which ones. If you can't figure it out, and you really, really want to know, send me a message on Facebook or Twitter and I'll clear it up for you.

Last, this book is a good bit shorter than my previous work. For example, *No Easy Hope* was 116,000 words, roughly, while this novel weighs in at about 60,000. Still novel length, but more concisely written than my other books.

Now that I have armed you with all the pertinent information necessary to make an informed buying decision, let me just say that I sincerely hope you buy this novel. Not just because I write for a living, and if you don't buy it I might have to start eating Top Ramen every day, but because Joshua and I devoted a lot of time and effort to it and we are both proud of the work we did here. It is a fast paced, engaging story with lots of gore, action, and heart: the holy trinity of post-apocalyptic storytelling. We think you will like it.

As always, thank you for all your support and encouragement, and for letting me live my dream. You, awesome reader, are the reason I do this. Without you, I'm just another lame dude pecking away at a keyboard.

You keep reading them, and I'll keep writing them.

James N. Cook

Charlotte, NC

July 28th, 2013

Foreword

By Joshua Guess

Some of you know who I am—after all, this book is half my work, so I've shared it with my own readers—but some of you don't. Rather than bore you with a bunch of biographical details, I'd rather use this space to tell you why I enjoyed this project so much.

A large part of it was the chance to work with James (Jim) Cook. A year ago today, Jim interviewed me for his blog, and I learned that while we are remarkably similar people, we have very different writing styles. Different, but strangely complimentary. James came up with the idea of collaborating on a standalone Surviving the Dead novel, and in late May of this year, we got started.

I've been writing for half my life, diligently working to develop my abilities. Jim, however, didn't start until he was 30 years old. That impressed the hell out of me; *No Easy Hope* does not read like a first try. I know, I have a file full of false starts and half-finished manuscripts. When he approached me about writing *The Passenger*, I was excited. Jim has a big audience—that's you—and he told me he wanted help me reach full-time status as an author.

That meant a lot to me. I've worked very hard to get where I am, but I always told myself (and my wife, Jess) that I would stay working until I had the income from writing to go full-time. In March of this year, when our tax returns came in, I broke that promise. There were many factors in that decision, but mostly, I realized I needed the time off from working to put all my efforts into my next book. My dream has always been to do this for a living, and thanks to Jim, who put the first chapter of that novel, *Victim Zero*, at the end of his most recent book *Warrior Within*, I'm now a full-time writer.

It's been life changing.

The book you're about to read matters to me for a lot of reasons. One is the obvious: it will make me money. Funds I can use to pay the bills and keep writing. Another is the challenge it represented. When writing my own books, I'm free to do anything. But I find myself creating purposeful restraints that force me to be creative. The restraints I faced in writing *The Passenger,* and the challenges it created, were twofold: I had to write in a universe not my own, and I had to write from a perspective strongly limited by the context of the story. I think doing so made me more creative, and more original.

Beyond the royalties and their ability to help me write full-time, beyond the craft aspects of the work itself and how they helped me become a stronger writer, and even past the excellent complimentary structure of the story which contrasts my style and Jim's, I got to make a friend.

Before we started working on this book, Jim and I were friendly, but distant. Over the course of the project, we became friends. We talked on the phone regularly as we worked out the story, which led to entertaining conversations and general bullshitting. I'm not saying we braided each other's hair or anything, but our professional relationship became a strong friendship. When Jim came to Kentucky to finish up the book in person, my mom even gave him a hug.

It was good times. All of it.

Every writer who manages a career out of putting words on paper gets there a different way. Jim struck gold with his first book, finding success almost right away. And he deserved it. His work is strong, his books are entertaining and gripping, and he didn't get lazy. If anything, his dedication to putting out ever-better books as well as interacting with his fans is even stronger now.

Although I've been at it longer, I haven't been as lucky as others. I've had good times, but no explosive popularity. Instead, I've built my audience slowly, brick by brick. It's been hard work, and satisfying for that. But Jim's generous offer to help speed that along is awesome in the truest sense of the word.

At the end of the day, I'm happy even if this book sells not a single copy. I got a lot out of the experience, the best part being someone I can talk to about the business we're in, a friend who like all good friends will help me succeed as much as he can. Should my career suddenly blast off tomorrow, I would return the favor in a heartbeat.

The last few months have been exciting and scary and a million other things, but above all, they've been productive. The freedom to work on this project, the chance to spend more than a paltry few hours at the keyboard, is the best. Not because of the money, which has always been only a means to pay the bills, but because I get to tell the stories I've always wanted to tell. I get to entertain.

And in this case, *we* get to do that. The book you're about to read is a contrast in styles. It's dark. It's harsh. It brushes the coat of grime away from the raw nerve of human brutality. It forces you to deal with the worst things a person can do when there are no more checks and balances.

I had so damn much fun writing it. I hope you like reading it just as much.

Joshua Guess

Author, Doughnut Enthusiast, and Secret Adamantium-Laced Mutant Hero

Frankfort, Kentucky

July 29th, 2013

For Josh and Jacob.

Brothers, warriors, men of strength.

Wear your scars with pride, for you are not among the timid.

It is an honor to be your friend.

ONE

I've heard it said that dying is easy.

Some philosophers liken it to being born again, and indeed, many religions state it in those terms explicitly. I'm not a philosopher myself, but I have an advantage over them—I've been there. As the old saw goes, dying is easy. Living is hard.

Reanimating is a different ballgame altogether.

You remember it. It's not like being born in the sense that your awareness develops over time, the memories of blind panic crushed into singularity by the years of consciousness that come later. I remember it all. I was a man, once. I had a job, a family. I had a mortgage, and a nice car, and a collection of ties that had taken years of curating to get *just* right.

I had a name. I swear I did.

The one blessing that came with my death was that it was quick. I remember trying to escape the violence, swarms of undead being cut down by men in uniforms behind me. My family made it through the barricade ahead of me. As I moved through, one of those *things* managed to snag my hand. There was pain. I looked back to see the last two fingers on my right hand gone.

Even then, we knew what a bite meant. There was no time for worry or fear. I spent most of my adult life as a man who never had a chance to make a stand or be brave, but I did at that moment. My family looked at me as I clutched that wounded limb, the soldiers around us staring as they finished the cleanup.

I knew the options. I'd heard them enough times to feel the words indelibly burned into my mind. I could go easy and quick, or I could wait it out. Suffer, burn, die anyway. Then come back.

I didn't think about it for long. I rushed forward to kiss them goodbye, whispered a request to the soldier closest to me, and then ran back through the barricade as fast as my feet would take me. The bites could kill quickly, very quickly. I didn't want to be a danger to my family, or other people lucky enough to escape the swarm unharmed.

There weren't many undead left outside the barricade, and every one of them was moving in the opposite direction. Knowing I was already dead gave me a recklessness I wouldn't have risked otherwise. The few infected that came close enough to almost touch me were kicked or shoved in my desperate attempt to get far enough away that my family wouldn't see me fall.

I was maybe a hundred feet from the barricade when the shot rang out. It took me high in the shoulder, proving that not all marksmen are created equal. The push of the bullet threw me off balance, and I hit the ground at the edge of a small hill. Tail over teakettle, I rolled and thrashed through brush and debris. I heard my clothes tear against a hundred small obstructions; felt the damaged muscle and sinew in my upper back scream at the brutal earth every time I slammed against it.

The trip down the side of the hill seemed to last forever, but finally, it ended. My last memory as a living man was lying half-submerged in a babbling stream. It was cold. *I* was cold. I listened to the crack of gunshots slow down and eventually fade away. I looked up at the sky and wondered how I'd missed the beauty of the stars for all those years.

Funny, I thought. *Only at the twilight of humankind, when all the lights have gone out, do I finally see the lovely vastness that's always been there. Just beyond the border of my cluttered little life.*

And then I died.

*****

My body woke up before I did.

I don't know if it works that way for the other shambling corpses that make up my current peer group, but my first memory of my new life was coming to sudden and unfortunate consciousness as my body shredded the throat of a screaming man. My instinct was to pull away in horror, but I couldn't. In fact, I couldn't even look away.

I was a passenger. Read-only reality.

I railed and struggled to stop what my body was doing, to no avail. My hands—look there, that's my wedding ring, done in white gold inlays on tungsten carbide—pulled gobbets of flesh from what became a corpse during my struggles.

The full spectrum of sensory data was there, but I had no control over any of it. You can't imagine what it's like. It's not the same as watching some horrific television show you can't turn off. You're actually a part of the program. I felt the hot blood of the dead man running down my fingers. I smelled the sour perspiration on his skin. I heard his bowels cut loose, could taste the warm, salty meat of him as my estranged fingers jammed pieces into my mouth.

After an hour or so of eating and doing the mental equivalent of vomiting inside my own head, I heard something that filled me with hope: gunfire. The area we were in was unfamiliar, so I couldn't be sure if the shooters were soldiers or unsuspecting survivors. Briefly, I wondered how far my errant body had traveled under its new management, but gave up that curiosity when I realized it didn't matter. Wherever I had roamed, I hoped it was far enough away that my family wouldn't chance upon me. I didn't want them to see me this way.

Whoever was firing that gun had a chance to end this for me. My body was already moving toward the sound of the shots.

My God, the shots.

The *sound.*

The best way I can describe it is like hearing in 3-D. Something about the sonic waves ricocheting from the sharp crack of the rifle was akin to depth perception, but far more powerful. I just *knew* the direction it came from, the distance. Like knowing how to grab a ball from the air as it's thrown to you. Whatever the plague destroying humanity was, whatever it had done to me, it seemed to make my body a better predator.

I just hoped whoever I was heading toward was better still.

TWO

"Staff Sergeant, secure that weapon."

Ethan heard his commanding officer, but didn't turn to look. His heart was beating too fast in his chest, his blood too loud in his ears to register the command. Numbly, he stepped forward, his legs on autopilot.

"Thompson! What the hell are you doing?"

He kept walking. Step by agonizing step, he got closer to the revenant. It was face down on the ground, partially coagulated blood seeping from an exit wound on the back of its head. It was the right height, the right build, even the hair color was the same. Dark brown, peppered with gray, grown down to the shoulders. Ethan stopped next to the body and reached down to roll it over with a trembling hand.

"Hey, Ethan. You all right man? The fuck are you doing?"

Dimly, he recognized Justin's voice. His friend's footsteps crunched in the frost as he came closer. Ethan rolled the body onto its back and leaned down to study its face. After a long instant, his shoulders sagged, and a fog rose around his head as he let out a breath.

"It's not him."

"What?"

Ethan looked up. "It's not him."

Justin's face registered understanding. He kneeled down and placed a hand on the big man's shoulder.

"Of course it's not him. Your old man's too tough to end up like that. He's still out there somewhere. Maybe we'll find him in Tennessee."

Ethan nodded slowly, and got back to his feet. Lieutenant Jonas was striding toward the two of them, his face tight with irritation. "You two wanna tell me what the fuck you're doing?

In case you didn't notice, the platoon is getting ready to move out."

Ethan pointed at the corpse with his pistol. "Sorry, sir. I thought I recognized this one."

Jonas planted his hands on his hips and glared. "I don't give a damn if you thought it was Kate Upton with her tits hanging out. The order was weapons safe. Did you forget what that means in the last two minutes, Staff Sergeant?"

"No sir."

"Then secure that goddamn sidearm and get your squad ready to move." The lieutenant turned and stalked off.

Ethan unscrewed the suppressor from his Beretta M-9 and stowed it on his belt, then replaced the pistol in its holster. He turned to walk back to the bivouac, but Justin put a hand on his arm and stopped him.

"Dude, hold up a second."

He looked down and watched as Justin shoved the gun all the way into his chest rig until it locked into place. The holster didn't have a strap, just a thumb paddle that he depressed as he drew his weapon. It was attached to a MOLLE vest, along with spare magazines, a first aid kit, fighting knife, multi-tool, a canteen of water, and a short-handled fire axe.

"You must really be out of it, man. Get any sleep last night before you took the watch?"

Ethan sighed, and shook his head. "Not much. Too damn cold."

"I hear you." Justin pulled a small brown packet from his vest. "Here, you can have the coffee pack from my MRE. Might help you wake up."

Ethan almost said no, but then thought better of it and reached out. "Thanks."

Walking the short distance back to his two-man tent, he saw SPC Derrick Holland staring contemptuously at him. The short, compact soldier had a smirk on his narrow face, and addressed Ethan with his usual insolence. "Nice work, Sergeant. One shot, one kill. I hate to be the one to tell you this, but that's a pistol." He pointed at the Beretta. "And that's a hand weapon." He pointed at Ethan's axe. "We're supposed to be using blades to kill the Rot. Not guns."

Ethan brushed past him. "Shut your face, Holland. Is your fire team ready to move out?"

"Will be in about five minutes."

"You've got two. Make it happen."

Holland chuckled, and started toward Cormier and Hicks. "Let's go fellas. Staff Sergeant is in a mood today."

Ethan glared after him, his right hand squeezing into a fist. Holland had been in the Army since before the Outbreak, but unlike most soldiers from that era, he hadn't climbed very far up the ranks. His insubordinate attitude and disregard for the strictures of discipline had cost his career dearly. Ethan had gotten along well with Holland before being promoted to sergeant. Ever since then, however, Holland had been a resentful little shit. But for all that, Ethan had to admit Holland was a good soldier. He had plenty of combat experience and, despite his low rank, he knew how to keep his head in a fight. Furthermore, his skill with a rifle had earned him the distinction of being the squad's designated marksman. He was a pain in the ass for sure, but a good man to have around when things got messy.

"You're going to have to do something about that little bastard," Justin said, stepping up behind him. "I've about had it with him giving you lip all the time."

Ethan glanced at his friend, and not for the first time, he was taken aback at how much Justin had changed. Two years ago, he had been a gangly, awkward nineteen-year old just emerging from the scalding battlefield of adolescence. Since then, life in the Army had put twenty pounds of muscle on his frame, and long exposure to wind and sun had weathered his once boyish face. Bright, intelligent blue eyes stood out in stark contrast to his tanned skin and blond hair.

"What do you want me to do?" Ethan said. "Article 15? We're out in the shit, it's cold as balls, and Fort Bragg is about a hundred miles that way." He raised a hand and pointed eastward. "I need Holland focused and motivated, same as everybody else. If giving me a hard time keeps his morale up, I've got thick enough skin to take it."

"He's just going to keep fucking with you," Justin replied. "I know his type. I dealt with assholes like him all the time in high school. He'll keep pushing your buttons until you do something about it. You need to put him in his place. If you don't, then I will."

Ethan smiled, and stepped closer to the younger man. "Listen, I appreciate your loyalty, but I don't need you fighting my battles for me. Holland is my responsibility, not yours. If he gets out of hand, I'll deal with it. But the absolute *last* thing I need is you starting a fight within the squad. We're going into combat soon, and God only knows how long we'll be in Tennessee. We can't have good order and discipline breaking down less than a week into the deployment. Okay?"

Justin frowned, but nodded. "All right."

Ethan patted him on the arm before getting to work breaking down his tent. A short time later, his nine-man squad was packed up and ready to move out. As usual, they were the first ones finished.

"Get a move on ladies," Jonas shouted, striding through the encampment. "Delta's already got their shit together. What's taking the rest of you so long?"

Jonas stopped beside Sergeant First Class Damian Ashman and glared pointedly at the tall, powerfully built man. "Maybe I should make Thompson platoon sergeant. At least he can get his people up and moving in a timely manner."

Ashman took the rebuke in stride, and turned to his men. "Last man on the rails gets the mid-watch and latrine duty for the next five days."

Lieutenant Jonas stared on in mute satisfaction at the ensuing scramble.

Ethan watched them with a thin smile, and then turned to look at the railroad tracks a short distance away. There, straddling the rails, was a vehicle the likes of which the young soldier had never seen before, at least until a few weeks ago.

The people who arrived with it had called themselves Facilitators. Forty men and twenty-four women, all wearing the same dark coveralls with the words PHOENIX INITIATIVE stenciled on the back. With them came a myriad of blocky, utilitarian machinery. Small generators that could run on almost any kind of fuel, even whiskey. Larger generators filled with water and steam pipes that turned biomass into electricity. Vehicles powered by the same technology that looked more like farm tractors than transport vehicles. And of course, the U-trac. Not a train, mind you. An abbreviation of MK 850 Railway Utility Tractor. U-trac.

The one down the hill from Ethan was squat, square, and roughly the size of a minivan. A small operator's compartment sat on top, and behind it, a convoy of scaled-down train cars covered close to forty yards of track. The first few cars coupled behind the engine were simple boxes designed to carry ammunition, equipment, and fuel. Behind these sat the passenger carriages, which were smaller than those found on standard trains, and designed with function in mind rather than comfort. Arrow-slit windows lined the armored walls while hatches allowed access to the roof, and there were even trap doors installed in the floor in case something blocked the other exits. Ethan concluded that whoever had built the things had put a great deal of thought into their design.

"Let's go, gentlemen," Ethan said, gesturing at his subordinates. "Stow your gear and take a seat."

The troops in his squad grumbled under their breath, none of them looking forward to another uncomfortable, monotonous day riding the rails. Nevertheless, they did as they were told. It was always this way with soldiers, Ethan had learned. They might bitch and moan, but they did their jobs.

The nine men of Delta Squad lifted their worldly possessions onto their backs and walked down the hill to the U-trac. They stowed their large, modular MOLLE packs in the cargo hold, but held on to their rifles and their smaller, cylindrical assault packs. Go-bags, they called them. If something happened to the engine and the soldiers had to bug out in a hurry, the go-bags were supposed to hold the minimum of equipment they would need to survive. The Army even provided a list of everything they were supposed to have in them, and it was Ethan's job to make sure they abided by it.

That was the rule, anyway.

Whoever had written the book on how to stock a go-bag had clearly never spent any time out in the shit. Which meant that Ethan flagrantly and unapologetically disregarded that particular set of regulations, as did the other squad leaders. Mostly, their go-bags were full of batteries, toilet paper, a couple of days' worth of food, and most importantly, ammo. Like all survivors of the Outbreak, they had learned that being armed was far more important than being fed. A soldier could live for a month without food. But without a weapon, it was unlikely any of them would last more than a day.

Once their equipment was secured, the soldiers filed into the first passenger carriage directly behind the command car. They chose this car over the others for two reasons. First, it was in the middle. If any insurgents had set up IED's along the railway, they would most likely try to blow the engine and the last car in order to trap the U-trac in place. If that happened, being in the middle gave them the best chance of survival. Second, it was far enough away from the engine's exhaust that they wouldn't have to breathe in suffocating JP8 fumes. Ethan had once remarked to his men that jet-fuel exhaust smelled like hot vinegar and sorrow. No one had disagreed.

The U-trac, much like an Abrams tank, had multi-fuel capability, giving it the ability to run on a variety of combustible fluids. JP8 jet-fuel was in plentiful supply at Pope AFB—shipped in from vast strategic reserves in Kansas—so that was what they used.

Inside the passenger car, a single, wide bench sat welded to the middle of the floor. Delta Squad filed in and sat down on either side, back to back. There was enough room for twelve people if they packed in, but since First Platoon only consisted of four squads, they each got a carriage to themselves. Ethan took a seat in the middle with Justin on one side, and Sergeant Isaac Cole on the other. Cole—all six-foot-four, two-hundred seventy pounds of him—was the squad's heavy gunner.

"Man, I'll be glad when we done with this shit," Cole said, turning his head Ethan's way. "I'd rather be fighting the Rot than sittin' here freezin' my black ass off."

Justin leaned forward. "Hey Cole, you're from Tennessee, right?"

"Yeah."

"So isn't this kind of like a homecoming for you?"

Cole grinned. It was the kind of smile that made young women blush and old women laugh. Ethan had seen it in action many times, to devastating effect. "Man, you know I joined the Army to get the hell *out* of Tennessee, right? You ever been to Memphis?"

Justin shook his head.

"Well, let me tell you something 'bout Memphis. Just 'cause Elvis from there don't mean it's all sunshine and flowers and shit. There used to be some hard-ass neighborhoods up in Memphis. Places where if you showed up and you ain't have yo' ghetto pass, you a mu'fuckin' dead man."

Ethan said, "You do realize we're not going anywhere near Memphis. Right?"

Cole shrugged. "Don't matter. It's still Tennessee. All these years I spent stayin' the hell away from that place, and now I gotta go back. If my ass gets killed there, I'm a' be pissed."

Ethan thought about asking the big gunner why he hated Tennessee so much, but there was something in Cole's expression that stopped him. A weight of pain that was out of character for the jovial soldier. Ethan met his gaze for a moment, then nodded and looked away. Cole was quiet after that.

The sun began to break over the horizon as the other squads straggled in and began filling up the remaining carriages. The U-trac's engineer—a surly civilian contractor who gave only a hostile 'Gus' when asked for his name—took his seat in the operator's box and began doing pre-operation checks. Ethan watched Lieutenant Jonas walk the line of cars and ask the squad leaders if all their men were present and accounted for. When the lieutenant stopped by his car, he gave the usual bored affirmative.

Finished with his checks, Lieutenant Jonas—a former master sergeant who had been given a field commission shortly after the Outbreak—climbed into the car ahead of Ethan's, radioed a mission update to Fort Bragg, and motioned to Gus to get the U-trac moving. Hydraulic accumulators whined, the massive motor rumbled to life, and with a blast of exhaust and a screech of brakes releasing, the engine lurched forward. Ethan and his men rocked to the side as their car jerked into motion, their expressions unmoved.

The young NCO looked through a narrow window to the northwest. The CSX line they were following would take them another hundred miles to a series of short lines, and from there they would pick up the Norfolk Southern track toward Albemarle and Salisbury. But first, they had to get through Hamlet. Ethan had heard a lot of things about Hamlet from other soldiers who passed through there.

None of it had been good.

THREE

The thing about walking places is that it takes time.

For the average person, this is not a problem. Walking for pleasure is one of those activities that harkens back to the nomadic roots of humanity. For tens of thousands of years, we ambled along from one place to another, our feet taking us on the hunt for herds of buffalo and babbling springs. Something in us wants to move, to feel the earth turn beneath us and watch the landscape change. Many people walk for pleasure: hikers, people trying to get or stay healthy, or just folks who appreciate nature.

I've never been one of those. When I was still alive, I only walked when I had to.

In death, my body lacked the coordination of the healthy human form. It stumbled all over the place, weaving back and forth with the contours of the ground. Though the destination was clear in my mind, shared with me by the strange, hungry reptile brain in charge of my limbs, the path from point A to point B was less than straight. Think of it more like a wobbly arrow. Drunk people have more coordination.

The result was that it took a long time. I spent a great deal of it trying to wrest back control of my limbs before finally giving it up as impossible. Then followed several hours of trying to rest only to discover that whatever force keeping my mind running inside my cramped skull lacked the requirements of a healthy brain, thus preventing me from sleeping. As much as I wanted to check out, I was forced to endure the endless monotony of walking. There are many possibilities you might expect after death. Funny that boredom was never on my list.

The day didn't drag by. That descriptor leaves too much leeway. It makes the experience appear to inhabit the same universe as tolerable. It didn't. The day scraped by like a hundred pieces of jagged metal slowly pulled across broken asphalt. The slow, unchanging pace of it was maddening, nails on a chalkboard for hours without end.

Have you ever tried to put yourself to sleep? Maybe you thought about something distracting like a business proposal or a book you'd been reading? After enough mind-numbing boredom, any distraction begins to appeal and I tried as many as came to mind.

What stood out most was the way the broad strokes of my life were plain to see—the office, the daily drive to work, the constant stress of looking busy in case the boss came by while secretly entertaining myself with video games—yet the details were absent. Some were there, if very fuzzy, but by and large, empty spaces took up what should have been important things.

What spurred this realization was the fact that my dead body had inherited some of my living body's mannerisms. My son—damn it, I should know his name—used to give me a hard time about the way my arms swing when I walk. Called me a gorilla. My body kept that habit, and with every step, I could see my wedding ring flash in the light. I thought about the wedding, tried to focus on it as a distraction, but it was like peering through a gauzy curtain. Which was when I began to understand how far the voids in my recollection went.

My wife's name, my son's, the country where we spent our honeymoon … gone. So many little things evaporated from my brain like so much water on a hot summer day.

But the emotions, Jesus. The way I felt when I kissed her at the altar for the first time, the thrill of joy when the doctor raised my firstborn in front of me and smacked him on his wee ass. Those sense-memories were still there, but somebody had cranked the saturation level up to eleven. The feelings were so strong it was as if no time had passed at all.

Faced with nothing but the long walk ahead of me, I dove without hesitation into the wide and deep abyss of times past, wallowing in sensations untouched by the fog of experiences between. I explored everything I could think of. Not just the pleasant, but every part of the spectrum. Joy, sadness, hard laughter, and bitter tears. The birth of my children, and the death of my parents. As my body trundled on toward some unknowable but certainly terrible destination, I swam the waters of memory and basked in the highs and lows of what came before.

In this horrific pseudo-death, however long it might last, I resolved to remember life. My body could control the physical aspects of my behavior, but even as I sobbed in remembered pain, I made a promise that none of the horrors sure to come would make me forget who I was.

A promise like that is always an exercise in foolishness—made in earnest, and guaranteed to be broken.

FOUR

The trouble started, as it usually did, with the crack of a rifle.

A high-powered one by the sound of it, Ethan thought. The bullet smashed into the operator's compartment on the U-trac, and if not for the four inches of ballistic glass between Gus and the rest of the world, his head would have burst like a melon. As it was, the grizzled engineer barely flinched.

"Looks like we got company."

Ethan looked at Cole to find him grinning broadly. The handsome man's smile faltered, however, when more rifles fired and nearly a dozen rounds broke themselves against the armor of their passenger car. Ethan snatched up his rifle and leapt to his feet.

"Against the wall!" he shouted.

Delta squad surged up from the bench and fanned out against the two-inch thick steel walls standing between them and whoever it was firing on the U-trac. Ethan peered out the narrow window and looked across the tall grass separating the tracks from the treeline less than a hundred yards away. As he watched, the branches parted and swirled, and over a dozen horsemen broke cover and began driving their mounts hard toward the slow-moving transport. The riders stood up in their saddles, knees bent with boots locked into stirrups, leveled their rifles, and began firing.

"Goddammit, how'd they know we were coming?" Cole shouted.

"You see they have horses, right?" Ethan replied. "Probably a patrol spotted us and then rode back to get their friends. This shit-heap we're riding only goes about fifteen miles an hour."

Cole nodded understanding just as another volley of gunfire peppered the wall.

"*Fuck*," Ethan swore. It was only a matter of time until one of those rounds found its way through a firing port, and when that happened, the ricochet would rip them to pieces. *Got to make these assholes back off.*

"Cole, get that SAW up the ladder. Schmidt, Holland, Cormier, lay down cover fire until he can get the hatch open. Fuller, Page, Hicks, cover the other side. Shoot anything that fucking moves. Smith, make sure Cole doesn't run out of ammo."

Private Smith stood ashen-faced against the wall, sweating bullets in spite of the cold and clutching his rifle with trembling hands. Looking at him, Ethan remembered his own first taste of combat. The lurching in his stomach, the pounding of his heart, the rasp of his own rapid, panicky breath grating in his ears. There was only one cure for that ailment, and that was to get into the fight.

"Smith! You fucking deaf?"

He jerked and looked at Ethan, the whites of his eyes round and bulging. "Yeah. I mean no. I mean…I hear you, Sergeant. I got it." He shuffled over to a dull metal case mounted against the wall, flipped the latch, opened it, and took out a green box of belted 7.62mm NATO ammunition. As he did so, Cole hefted his M-240 Squad Automatic Weapon—or just SAW, as it was more commonly known—and stepped up the short ladder leading to the roof. He turned the handle to unlock it, but stayed bent beneath the hatch.

"All right, open fire!" Ethan shouted. He leveled his rifle through the narrow firing port and began squeezing off rounds. The riders were approaching fast and firing as quickly as they could. Try as he might, Ethan couldn't get a good shot at any of them. Behind him, he heard Justin, Cormier, and Holland open fire as well.

"Got one!" Holland shouted.

As Ethan watched, one of their pursuers slumped over and fell from his saddle. His boot lodged in the stirrup as his horse continued to gallop along, dragging his limp, flailing body across the ground. The riders behind the dead man saw what happened to him and began to back off. The ones in front, oblivious to their cohort's fate, continued their pursuit. One of them came level with the wheels of the rear car, reached into a saddlebag behind him, and produced some kind of improvised explosive. A very large one.

Where the hell did he get that? Ethan couldn't get the man in his sights, so he shifted his aim lower and squeezed off a short burst. The man's mount screamed as several rounds tore into its lower chest and the thick muscles of its legs. The animal pitched forward, rolling and thrashing and crushing its hapless rider. As he fell, the bomb went flying and detonated several yards behind the U-trac's rear wheels.

"They've got some kind of grenades!" Ethan shouted. "Isaac, time to earn your paycheck!"

Cole's teeth stood out sharp and white. "Hell to the yeah, baby."

He pushed the hatch open with one meaty hand, surged up through the opening, and leveled his SAW.

"WHOOOOO YEAH MOTHERFUCKER!"

Short, staccato bursts of fire began pouring from the heavy weapon, tearing into the approaching riders and sending them tumbling to the ground in screaming, bloody heaps. Some of the rounds went low and caught the horses, but there wasn't much Cole could do about that. The SAW wasn't the most accurate weapon in the world.

At the same time, the squads riding in the other passenger cars finally got it together and began adding their rifles to the fray. Whatever the raiders had been expecting when they set out to pursue the U-trac, it hadn't been hardened soldiers cutting them to ribbons with a withering hail of hot lead. Panicked, the ones still alive veered their mounts around and pounded away back toward the cover of the trees.

"Aw, come on now, get back here bitches. You know you LOOOOOVE this shit!"

The big gunner fired a final burst at the retreating marauders before stepping down and closing the hatch behind him. Cole's face glowed with excitement. Ethan shook his head.

"Nice work, gentlemen. You too, Smith."

The young private was still standing by the ladder clutching his box of ammo. "Me? I didn't do shit."

Ethan stepped forward and clapped him on the arm. "Sure you did. I gave you an order and you followed it. You didn't freeze up, or panic." He leaned forward with a conspiratorial whisper. "You didn't shit yourself, did you?"

Smith let out a nervous laugh. "No."

Ethan stood up straight and grinned at the younger man. "Then you did just fine. Maybe next time I'll even let you do some of the fighting."

Smith's smile grew sickly, then disappeared altogether.

The door at the far end of the car opened and Lieutenant Jonas stepped through the narrow opening, careful not to step into the short length of empty space separating the command car from Delta's passenger carriage. "Everyone all right in here? Anybody hurt?"

"No sir," Ethan replied. "We're all good." He turned to Smith. "Check the other cars for me, private. Find out if there are any casualties."

Smith nodded. "I'm on it."

As the private hustled to the next adjoining car, Jonas stepped closer to Ethan. "Did my eyes deceive me, or were those raiders on horseback?"

"Yes sir, they were."

The lieutenant ran a hand over the back of his neck, his mouth forming a thin, hard line. "Well, ain't that just fucking wonderful. How much you want to bet those sons of bitches are from Hamlet?"

"I'm not a betting man, but I'd say your odds are pretty good, sir."

"And now they have bombs." Jonas shuffled over to a window and planted a hand against the wall as he stared out. "We're the first U-trac to come out this way, Thompson. And now they've seen us. I guaran-damn-tee you that by tomorrow these tracks are going to be lousy with IEDs. Fucking Hamlet. Place is a goddamn den of thieves, and slavers, and insurgent scum. I've got half a mind to radio for permission to go root those fuckers out."

Ethan watched the older man move to the bench and sit down, back straight. He looked incongruous with just a single bar on his collar. Most of the officers his age had oak leaves or silver eagles with wings spread wide. It was easy to forget that Jonas had spent most of his career in the Army as an enlisted man, working his way up the through the ranks the hard way. He'd seen more than his share of combat, and wasn't afraid to take up arms and get in the thick of things when the situation required it. Because of this, and his deep understanding of the needs and concerns of his soldiers, Ethan trusted and respected him, as did the other men. Nevertheless, the idea of walking blindly into hostile territory—and going off mission to do it—struck Ethan as not being the best of ideas.

"What about Pope? Maybe they could send out a drone to recon the place, find out what we're up against. I'm not afraid of a fight, sir, but I don't like going in blind. Not if we can help it, at least. There's no sense in getting ourselves killed needlessly."

A less experienced officer may have bristled at Ethan's suggestion, if not his tone. Jonas, however, nodded calmly. He knew good advice when he heard it, and he wasn't arrogant enough to think his experience precluded him from making mistakes. The Army had NCOs for a reason, after all.

"You're right, Sergeant, as usual. Still, knowing those fuckers are out there…"

Holland spoke up, "If you want LT, I can take a couple of guys and go scout it out. See what I can find. Maybe make some trouble for 'em."

Jonas thought about it for a moment, but shook his head. "No. I appreciate your courage, Holland, but I can't spare you. Besides, we're behind schedule as it is. We can't afford the delay."

The door to the car opened, and Private Smith stepped back through. "No casualties, sir. Everybody's okay."

Jonas stood up. "Good, good. Any fight you survive is a good one, right men?"

Delta Squad nodded in agreement, their faces grim as they remembered fights that not all of them had walked away from. Fights where they had lost friends, men who were so familiar, who had shared so much terror and hardship, that they were like family. Brothers, all of them. Private Smith shuffled his feet and remained silent. He had been assigned to Delta after his predecessor was killed in the line of duty. No one had told him the circumstances of the man's death, but he knew the other soldiers of First Platoon had taken the loss hard. And none harder than the men around him.

"You all did well," Jonas said. "That was a good, fast response. Especially you, Cole, you're a goddamn nightmare with that SAW."

The gunner grinned. "You know what they say, sir. Do what you love, and you'll never work a day in your life."

Jonas barked a short laugh. "Damn right. All right then, looks like we're squared away." He gestured at Ethan. "Staff Sergeant, round up the other squad leaders and get reports from them. Command is going to want to know what we just expended valuable ammunition on."

"Yes sir."

"The rest of you keep your eyes peeled for trouble. Holland, put that scope of yours to use and watch our back trail. Those raiders might find their spines and decide to pay us another visit. If they do, I want warning well ahead of time."

Holland nodded. "Want me to get the other DMs to do the same, sir?"

"No, just you and Sergeant Kelly for now. Rotate out with the other two in a couple of hours."

"Will do."

Ethan watched the lieutenant open the door and step back into the command car. He caught a glimpse of the cot along the wall, and the chair bolted to the floor in front of a small desk. It would have been mean accommodations under other circumstances, but standing there in the bare passenger car, he felt like a character in a Dickens novel staring through a window at Christmas dinner. The door shut, and the room was lost to view. He sighed, shoulders slumping.

Time to round up the other squad leaders. Time to write a report.

Goddamn, I hate paperwork.

*****

Hamlet passed by to the north of the U-trac much the same as any other town.

Ethan watched the outlines of buildings in the distance as they slowly drifted from left to right, little more than grey and brown husks against the blue morning haze. Even from this far away, he could see the empty, yawning holes staring out from behind shattered windows, the black scorch marks left behind by long-ago fires, and the sharp, stabbing fingers of I-beams, support struts, and shattered concrete pillars where office complexes and government buildings had once stood. All collapsed now. All reduced to great, mountainous heaps of forgotten rubble.

Across the depressing expanse between the town and the tracks, littered like corpses on a battlefield, lay houses, businesses, long-dead industrial facilities, and sagging structures that seemed to have no identifiable purpose at all. Every visible wall was crowded with vines and creepers that swarmed over rooftops in choking, skeletal tangles. Autumn's chill had turned everything brown and dead, and blanketed the landscape in an ocean of endless beige beneath a cloudy, pewter-colored sky. All seemed still. Abandoned. Quiet.

Ethan knew better.

There were eyes out there. Many eyes, and none of them friendly. They watched the tracks, he knew. They watched, and they would remember. He would not have been surprised if word of the brief, bloody firefight had already reached the marauders holed up in that shattered ruin of a town. Nor would it have surprised him to learn their plans for retaliation were already in motion. It was what they did, these marauder bands. They fought. They killed. They took from others. And if they were attacked, their response was never proportional, never just an eye for an eye. They were vicious, savage people with no regard for anyone's lives other than their own. Often, they even fought amongst each other, robbing, raping, and stealing.

It was a well-known fact in the Army that you didn't go after marauders with half measures. You didn't just hit them and hope they would learn their lesson. These were people who didn't back down from a fight. Didn't run away. Didn't get intimidated by the occasional strafing run or mortar bombardment. If a platoon was sent to take down known marauders, it wasn't just a police action. It wasn't just an effort to bring them to heel.

It was total annihilation.

Kill them all, root and branch, or die in the attempt. And dying wasn't outside the realm of possibility. More than once, entire platoons had limped back to Fort Bragg decimated and in shambles, most of their men dead or dying of wounds or infection. Contrary to what all the strategists had predicted, the marauders were becoming increasingly well-armed. Unexplainably, alarmingly so. They were determined, these insurgents and raiders, and they were getting better at their craft. And out there, across that cracked veneer of dead civilization, was an unknown number of them.

Waiting. Plotting.

Ethan stood near the wall, his face close to the chill, gently blowing air outside and stared out the narrow window as the U-trac slowly rattled along. He searched rooftops for movement, eyes narrowed, jaw constantly working. He searched the tall grass for the telltale streaks of lighter brown that would indicate someone having passed through recently. He breathed in deeply through his nose, trying to catch the acrid odor of wood smoke born on the wind. He listened for the crack of distant rifles echoing across the low, gently rolling hills. But mostly he simply watched, gaze unfocused, never letting his eyes rest on one spot for too long, determined to spot trouble if it was out there. He rested his head against one thick forearm, and for long into the morning, he watched.

He watched, and he worried.

FIVE

The swarm happened the way planets happen. Slowly, and over time, but inexorable. When the sun finally began to fade, from the corner of my eye, I noticed the presence of others like me.

Well, whether they were *really* like me is open to debate, but I can say for sure they were dead people. Ones who forgot that death is supposed to be a state of motionless finality. This particular group was anything but restful, ambulating with drunken grace toward the same distant signal to which my own battered form gravitated.

At first, I was alone. Or rather, alone with myself if that makes sense. After trying long enough, I'd discovered a way to keep my brain occupied, only to have that lovely vacancy shattered by the grinding shuffle of other walking corpses.

I couldn't see much, but there was no missing the intense focus on their faces. It wasn't a look shouting intelligence or cunning, it was base. As bestial as they come. The most basic human need...no, the most basic need, period.

Hunger.

Deep and grisly.

When I first woke up, it was in the middle of my body feeding itself. I shuddered at the memory, as crisp and clear as the rest, but there was no shared sense of desire with it. Now, however, half a day had passed, and the dire change that drove my physiology to crave the flesh of human beings was demanding fresh material to work with.

For the first time, I felt it. There was an odd twinning in my perception as the reptile part of me imagined biting through soft skin, no more odd than having an egg and a slice of bacon. The first, powerful reaction was one of benign normality. The sense that all was as it should be.

Then the intellectual reaction happened, and I screamed inside my skull.

In a desperate bid to ignore the hunger, I tried to take in my surroundings. Anything interesting, anything at all to take my mind away from the gnawing urge. The urge to gnaw.

I—or rather, my body—wandered, and as our feet ate up the miles, others appeared. Some of them were freshly dead, so new that if it weren't for the glaze over their eyes and the drunken lurch of their movements, you might not know they were corpses. Others, well…

Not so much.

A little girl came into view, ragged jeans and shirt flapping in the rising mist. At first, a pang of sadness rolled through me that a child should have to die, doubly that she should come back afterward. Then a random noise in the distance caused her to turn toward me, and I saw the other half of her.

I'm not being metaphorical here. On her right side, the side facing me, she looked like a perfectly normal (if very dead) child of about ten. The left side, however, was a mass of bites. She hadn't died easy. The skin on her face was stripped away, the bones of her cheek and jaw laid bare. The same grotesque story continued down her neck, which flexed wetly as she turned, gaping at me. Her left arm was gone, which, considering the damage, was probably a blessing.

There were others like her, the less fortunate dead who didn't get the mercy of even a badly placed bullet. Men and women with chunks of their flesh missing, limbs destroyed in an almost infinitely varied mosaic of sickening creativity. They weren't clean and tidy, these dead people. They were obviously, terribly dead. Walking billboards for the darkest aspects of predation.

More and more appeared. It was like some secret meeting, but whatever force drew us all together was not a part of my awareness. I felt the things my body felt, but as I watched the few become the many and the many become the swarm, I felt nothing. No pull, no incessant nagging to join with others. No inner radar telling me where to find more of the restless dead.

Nonetheless, they kept on coming. Maybe they were following that same strange directional sense I'd felt when the gunshots went off, but wherever the sound had come from, it had to have been left behind long since. I'd been walking almost all day, after all. Even a slow walker can cover a lot of distance in that time.

What was it, then, that drove my body forward? A scent trail I wasn't catching? Some subtle input I was unaware of? It had to be something. There was no way all these other ghouls were joining the party by sheer coincidence.

There was an intensity in the air, ephemeral but real. I felt it the way you know someone has walked into a room even when you can't hear or see them. There was a pressure to the air, the tension of a breath held for far too long. Alone, trapped inside my head, I had barely noticed it. But surrounded by the hungry dead it couldn't have been more obvious.

Hunger.

Deep, visceral need. The monster dwelling in my body responded to it, and my own (*not* mine, dammit) hunger responded in kind.

The group was headed for something, drawn to it like moths to a flame. As I pushed the sensation of hunger down, down, down into a place I didn't want to look, I hoped that, like moths that flew too close to the fire, I too would burn when I got there.

Now more than ever.

*****

My body wasn't relying on its higher functions to do any of the heavy lifting in a neurological sense, but its momma didn't raise no fool.

In front of the horde, now at least a hundred strong, lay a large creek. The creek itself wasn't the main problem; the steep drop that led to it was. The milling press of bodies drifted to and from the edge, every corpse in the crowd taking its turn contemplating the challenge before them as much as their withered gray matter would allow.

The sense of urgency faded somewhat when the way forward was blocked. I seriously doubted that would have been the case had some new stimuli reached our ears (or noses, or whatever), like gunshots or fresh blood. As it was, my body shuffled around the edge of the bank with all the others, locked in a holding pattern with no clear exit.

It was nighttime, and I realized my night vision was much more impaired than it had been during my life. Chalk it up to the vital functions stopping, I guess. The animating force that drove us, be it virus or voodoo, seemed to have its limitations. One of the many sacrifices made, apparently, was the involuntary ocular adjustment to darkness.

Denied the ability to sleep, which in my current state might technically be death, I grew frustrated. As unnerving as it was to share all the sensory information with my body while having zero control over it, finding myself essentially blinded was driving me crazy. I wasn't sure how much longer I could take it. I wanted to be wherever my body was heading because logic suggested there would be people there. My body and I both had a great desire for that, if for totally different reasons. People who had survived the Outbreak almost certainly knew how to defend themselves, after all, and I had high hopes that someone would kill me.

Funny how death can give you perspective on life, especially the quality thereof.

As I shuffled there in the darkness, the sudden, crystal-clear memory of my grandmother dying snapped into my mind. I remembered visiting her three times a week once the cancer reached the point where doctors somberly ask you to please step into the hallway. Three times a week, an hour at a time, I watched her die by inches.

At first, the cancer wasn't so bad; that's the great deception that comes with the disease. It's a liar, plain and simple. She felt bad, of course, which was what sent her to get checked in the first place. Hospice came soon after, even though she didn't feel quite like death yet.

But then came the progression. From being told she was dying, but being able to do things for herself, to actually *feeling* death begin to happen. Slow and steady, with a grip like iron, it came for her. Day by day she declined, mental faculties sharp, which given my current predicament I now saw as a curse.

She was in pain. So much that at one point she began asking me to end it. A lifetime of culture and society training you to think one way is difficult to break even when you're faced with the reality in front of you. I remember thinking that all she needed was another dose of medicine to get her through the rough parts. Another pain pill to take the edge off the jagged downward slope that was the end of her life. A life, I thought, that was as precious as any other, and not to be ended.

That complex of memories unfolded between heartbeats (or would have, if my heart had any life left in it) and a fresh wave of emotions came with it. But it was different now, tempered by my situation. Looking at her death as it came back to me, I wished she'd had a better end. The justifications and sad logic in my head were defense mechanisms, used to ignore the brightness of the truth: she was suffering, dying, and I watched it happen like some macabre reality show.

It seemed simple, in retrospect, ending the life of a person who knows the rest of her existence is going to be written in pain. A single terrible moment, the weight of guilt and responsibility heavy, but the results worth it. In the micro scale, it couldn't make more sense. But of course there were other considerations.

There was family to think about, and laws, and society, and on up the ladder until the size of the repercussions became too much to fight against. I remembered the months leading up to her death with grim discomfort, and then the relief I felt when I got the news of her passing. She got her end, finally, long and awful as the journey was. If there really is an afterlife, I'm sure the transition was a welcome reprieve.

I should be so lucky.

My reverie was interrupted suddenly by a commotion in the swarm around me. Bodies pushed back from the edge of the drop, forcing me to move back or be knocked over. An irregular scraping sound accompanied the wave of movement backward, followed by a splash. One of the others must have fallen off the bank of the creek.

The pressure on my body released as the tight mass moved forward. A symphony of faint grunts followed, along with the sound of dozens of bodies scraping against grass and dirt as well as the occasional dry crack of a bone breaking.

In front of me, the swarm was walking off the edge of the drop like stereotypical lemmings. As the way forward cleared, I saw one ghoul far out in front up to his waist in the water as he waded along. Interesting. The rest of them might not be great shakes in the brains department, but at least some remnant of problem-solving abilities had to exist. After all, they'd seen one of their fellows fall off and survive, then cross once he was in the water. Crude logic-

Sonofabitch!

The world tiled around me as I tried to throw my arms out to catch myself. It was off-putting to send out the familiar signals to my limbs and have them not respond in the slightest.

I'd distracted myself so much I hadn't paid attention to what my body was doing. Not that I could have changed it, but as my entire existence now seemed to revolve around my thoughts and only my thoughts, it seemed prudent not to allow myself to panic or be caught off guard. If the rest of my life's purpose was to simply abide and observe, I owed it to myself to at least do it right.

After all, I didn't have anything else.

SIX

By the time they stopped for the night, First Platoon had left the yellow zone behind and strayed deep into the red.

That was how they marked it on maps, the various concentrations of undead from one area to another, designated by the estimated number of infected per square mile. Green zones had twenty-five or less, yellow meant no more than a hundred, and red stood for anything beyond that. There was one other designation—black—reserved for major cities, large towns, and other areas where the infected were so thick that not even a large force of heavily armed troops with artillery, tanks, and air support would stand a chance. No one, not even the bravest, most bat-shit crazy of the human remnant went into the black. Not unless they *wanted* to die screaming in a swarm of ghouls.

Fort Bragg and most of surrounding Fayetteville were green. Not exactly a safe place to walk alone at night, but as long as people armed themselves and took a few sensible precautions, it was manageable. Yellow was hazardous, but survivable for the well prepared, making it prime scavenging territory. Red, however, was no fun at all. Nobody liked moving through red zones, not even marauders.

Ethan looked down at the map stretched out on the desk in the command car and felt his shoulders slump. *This shit never gets any easier, does it?* It was a new map, recently updated and given to them by a member of the Phoenix Initiative. The scientist who drafted it had used some kind of satellite thermal imaging technology to determine the location, density, and dispersion of the infected population throughout North Carolina and neighboring Tennessee. His findings were not encouraging.

"Did you spill a bottle of red ink on this thing, sir?" Ethan asked Lieutenant Jonas. "It's bleeding all over the place. I feel like I should go get a first aid kit."

Jonas chuckled, but there was no humor in it. He ran a finger westward from Salisbury to a region just west of the Tennessee River. "Sorry to say it, son, but we're in the shit from here all the way to Western Tennessee. I'm afraid the halcyon days of easy living and four-man watches are a thing of the past. We'll have to double the watches and start bedding down in the U-trac."

Ethan nodded grimly. He was just as tired as everyone else, and while he didn't relish the idea of double watches and sleeping in the cramped passenger carriages, he vastly preferred the additional hardship over having a hungry ghoul bite his face off in his sleep.

"I'll get the men to work on the braces and barricades," Ashman said, his head nearly scraping the ceiling of the command car. "You need me for anything else, sir?"

Jonas gestured around at Ethan and the other squad leaders. "Nope. Nothing these fellas can't handle."

The tall platoon sergeant nodded gratefully and stooped sideways to twist his bulk out of the command car. Once outside, he stood up straight and heaved a sigh, relieved to be out of the U-trac's cramped confines.

"Sergeant Kelly, I assume you've updated the watch rotation?" Jonas said.

Kelly nodded, the single light bulb in the ceiling gleaming on his bald head. He was a little shorter than Ethan, medium build, and like most of the men in First Platoon, sported a growth of reddish-blond beard that was forbidden by regulation. Razors were in short supply, even with the Army's resources, and soldiers in the field often hoarded them as valuable trade items. Once away from the insulated, spit-and-polish strictures of Fort Bragg, field units relaxed or altogether ignored many of the more cumbersome regulations heaped upon common soldiers. They had a hell of a lot more important things to worry about than the length of their hair, or the level of shine on their boots. Out in the wastelands, just staying alive from one day to the next was challenge enough.

"Already done, sir," Kelly replied.

"Very well. Thompson, you stick around for a minute. The rest of you, get this pig braced up and get your men situated. It's going to be a long, cold, shitty night. Do what you can to make your men comfortable."

The squad leaders nodded silently, all of them understanding the lieutenant's implied message. Officially, they weren't supposed to go scavenging except in life or death emergencies. By rule, salvageable goods were supposed to be left for civilians. The Army, after all, had far better access to basic necessities than the average Outbreak survivor scraping out a living in the wastes. However, every man in First Platoon was a seasoned campaigner, and they all knew the importance of making life as comfortable as possible in the field. Even something as simple as a scavenged blanket and a couple of dusty couch-cushions could make the difference between an aching back, and a good night's sleep. Ethan knew that fact all too well, having spent many a night sleeping on just such an arrangement. He also knew how important those kinds of things were to morale, and woe betide the squad leader who ignored them.

As soon as they were dismissed, Kelly and the other squad leaders called to their senior men and gave whispered instructions. Those men then went to their packs, retrieved weapons and ammunition, and informed First Sergeant Ashman that they were going out 'on patrol'. Ashman acknowledged them, knowing full well that their 'patrol' would most likely consist of searching the various nearby trailer parks, houses, abandoned businesses, and crashed vehicles for items worth dragging back to camp.

With the others gone, Ethan looked expectantly at Jonas. The lieutenant sat down in the chair in front of his desk and swiveled it around, sliding off his reading glasses. "Thompson, I want you to pick a few men, no more than three, and retrace our path back about a mile or so. I got a sneaky suspicion we ain't seen the last of those raiders. If they're out there, I want you to find them."

Ethan raised an eyebrow and stared for a moment. "Sir…if I may ask, why me? Sergeant Mallory is former SF. I know he's a little older, but he's still better suited for this kind of mission than I am."

"Sergeant Mallory is a good man, but he's forty-six and he's been out of Special Forces since the Clinton administration. It's why he's down here with the rest of us infantry grunts."

"What about Sergeant Kelly? He's been in since before the Outbreak. Did tours in Iraq. Why not him?"

Jonas' face darkened ever so slightly. "Are you turning chicken shit on me, Thompson?"

"No sir," Ethan replied evenly. "I'm just not sure if I'm the best man for the job."

Jonas stared searchingly for another moment before his expression softened. "Staff Sergeant, I want you to do this because my instincts tell me you *are* the right man. You have a nose for trouble, and your healthy sense of paranoia has pulled this platoon's ass out of the fire more than once. You're smart, you're cautious, and you're deliberate. That's what I need right now."

The lieutenant stood up, picked up a set of keys, and clapped Ethan on the arm. "And besides, the only way you're ever gonna get better at woodcraft is to practice. It's time for you to start stepping up and taking on more responsibility."

"Sir?"

"You might not have fought in the war, but unless I misjudge the situation, and I don't think I do, there's a whole other war brewing on the horizon. It's time for you to take the skills you've learned and start applying them."

Ethan frowned, more confused than ever. Jonas gave him a reassuring smile. "Come on, young man. Let's get a move on."

Jonas stepped outside, and Ethan followed. The lieutenant selected a key and unlocked one of the cargo containers just behind the U-trac's engine. The front of the container was completely black, and reeked of JP8 fumes. Jonas swung the doors open and selected a green plastic box from a shelf near the top.

"Here's four suppressors," he said, removing them and handing them to Ethan. "Make damned sure you bring them back. They're worth more than your life."

"Yes sir." Ethan reached out to take them.

Jonas closed the container and locked it. He took a few steps away and looked out over the assembly of soldiers carrying out their various tasks. Ethan followed his gaze, taking in the men's patched, threadbare uniforms, scuffed boots, scruffy hair and beards, and the hodge-podge of axes, crowbars, and other tools they had converted into melee weapons. Here and there, he saw soldiers who had supplemented their meager issue of uniforms with scavenged civilian clothes—gloves, scarves, hooded sweatshirts under their jackets, and name brand hiking boots. Wearing civilian clothes with their uniforms wasn't allowed, technically, but Jonas wasn't the kind of man make a soldier suffer the cold when there was something to be done about it. Ethan knew that not every CO was so lax, and he was grateful be in Jonas' platoon. In fact, he couldn't think of anyone else he would rather serve under.

"Was it like this before the Outbreak?" Ethan asked.

Jonas turned to look at him. "Like what?"

"This." Ethan gestured at the rest of the platoon. "Not ever having enough clothes, enough food, enough ammo. Not having enough of anything, really."

"Well, making due with damn little is nothing new," Jonas said with a chuckle, "but things weren't nearly this bad before the Outbreak. This platoon, these men, our gear, it's a shadow of what the Army used to be. Time was we could at least get new uniforms, although we had to pay for them, and there was enough food to go around. Now, well…things have changed. And not for the better."

The two men stood next to each other for a few seconds, silence stretching between them. Finally, Jonas said, "So who are you taking with you?"

Ethan glanced at his commanding officer, searching his face. From the slightly amused glint in the lieutenant's eye, he reckoned this was a test. Jonas was fond of tests, and quite often, the subjects of his scrutiny had no idea they were being tested until it was over with. He figured it best to err on the side of caution.

"Holland."

Jonas nodded. "Good choice. No brainer, that one. You're gonna need a sharpshooter."

Ethan scanned the men buzzing around the U-trac. Most of them were attaching bracing stanchions to the sides of the cars, similar to stabilizers on a crane. The stanchions were triangular bars that extended outward from the carriages and had flat, round feet hanging just a few inches off the ground. If the infected massed on one side of the U-trac or the other, the stanchions would keep the weight from derailing the cars or rolling them over. Additionally, the men were assembling a system of interconnecting steel bars fastened by mounting brackets welded to the carriages' frames. The bars formed a waist-high cage around the transport that would hold off the infected at about ten feet. All of the safety measures, braces and barricades alike, could be mounted or taken down in a matter of minutes. And none of them were anchored to the ground, which meant that if the U-trac needed to get going in a hurry, they didn't have to waste time dismantling their defenses. They could simply throw the engine in gear and take off. The countermeasures could always be removed later when they were out of danger.

One of the men working—a lean, wiry fellow with hollow blue eyes and a mess of scars on one side of his face—was busy pounding barricades together with a rubber mallet. He was the second newest member of Ethan's platoon, having only been with Delta Squad for six months. He rarely spoke, and when he did, it was with a thick Texas drawl. Several times, he had demonstrated an uncanny knowledge of wilderness survival, and often supplemented the platoon's meager rations with wild game he brought down with his M-4. An impressive feat, considering he didn't have a hunting scope.

"Hicks," Ethan said.

Jonas' eyebrows came together just a bit. "Hicks?"

"He's the best woodsman in the platoon. Quiet as a mouse, and he can shoot the nuts off a squirrel. He'll be my scout."

"All right then. Who else?"

"Cole."

Jonas turned to look at Ethan, amused. "Why Cole? Don't get me wrong, he's a good soldier, but he's also a wrecking ball. That really what you need for this mission?"

"Actually, sir, I'm hoping I don't need him at all. But if we're spotted, well...consider it an insurance policy."

The lieutenant grinned. "I like the way you think, Thompson. I really do." With that, he turned and strode away, leaving Ethan alone.

The young staff sergeant shuffled in place for a few seconds, not wanting to take the first step forward. If he did, he would have to round up his team and move out, after which they would be in the field, in the red zone, with an unknown number of enemy combatants possibly closing in on them. None of which filled Ethan with a sense of ease.

"Dammit Thompson," he muttered, forcing one foot in front of the other. "Don't just stand around pissing yourself. You're a soldier. Act like one."

A few minutes later, he and the three men he'd chosen moved off to the east and melted into the treeline. As Ethan wandered further and further away from camp, a dark uneasiness began to send cold tendrils whispering through his gut. He had felt it before, many times, but had never quite gotten used to it.

With his free hand—the one not clutching his rifle in a white-fingered grip—he reached up and touched his left chest pocket. The one with a picture of a bearded young man, about twenty pounds heavier, with a happy, unlined face, his arms around a beautiful red-haired woman. In the woman's arms was a baby, not yet six months old, but still obviously taking after his father. Same nose, same wide jaw, same dark brown eyes.

Holding the image in his mind, Ethan gritted his teeth and seized upon his fear, mastering it, making it his own. With hammer blows of determination, he melted it down, beat it into shape, and turned it into something else. Something his wife would not have recognized in the laughing, boisterous man she had married. It was something sharp. Something ugly.

Something deadly.

SEVEN

One advantage of being dead is that discomfort no longer applies, at least physically. The long, dark hours that night would have been unbearable for me as a living person, soaked to the skin and chilly as the air had to be. I say that without certainty because another of the important functions no longer in service was sensitivity to hot and cold.

It was there. It was just...well, shitty.

I could feel the wet bodies of the other ghouls rubbing up against mine, and though I could see the moisture and hear the wind dancing through the trees, I didn't get cold. I couldn't even feel the wind, which told me just how desensitized my body was.

Death was still a new ordeal for me, a gem with so many facets that it took time to even count them all much less examine each one. For example, it took me until that wet shamble up the other side of the creek to realize I no longer felt pain of any kind. While doing barrel rolls down the stony incline, I felt the pressure of the fall and the impacts all across my body, but it didn't hurt in the slightest. I would have chalked it up to luck had my hand not risen in front of my face after we left the creek, blindly feeling out for obstacles in the dense woods.

My right pinky was broken, and not in an 'oh, we're just going to set this and splint it' kind of way. Think industrial accident and you're getting warmer. Maybe my mind was just acclimating to the new way of things, but seeing my mangled finger flopping from my hand like a clown shoe didn't bother me at all. I found it rather fascinating, to tell the truth. I only wished I could fiddle with it, or at least move it closer.

I was caught completely off guard when the hand *did* move closer to my face. Not all the way in, but perhaps a few inches more toward my eyes.

Had I done that? I bent my will to the task of trying to move the hand closer, focusing everything I had on the image of my right hand arcing toward my face. If I could have controlled the necessary muscles, my face would have screwed up in concentration, teeth clenched, eyes narrowed.

Fucking hand didn't go anywhere, though. Probably just a coincidence. My body was prone to doing odd things, after all. Like dying and then going for a stroll. Mom always said my priorities were wrong.

My body stumbled onward, weighed down and off balance thanks to a gallon or two of creek water in its stomach and chest cavity. Though our tumble had been chaotic, I remembered the water going down my throat and into my lungs. Maybe a minnow or something went with it. The idea of a little life swimming around in there amused me until a few seconds later when I realized it would be certain death for the poor little fishy.

The wet slog that followed was boring but not terribly long. Soon enough, a pinprick of light appeared in the distance. It didn't have the steady burn of an electric bulb. It danced, flickering dim to bright in a wavering cycle. A campfire, maybe, if it was far away. A candle if it was closer. A single point of brightness in the night.

One part of me yearned for it, to be sitting near a warm fire. Another recognized the hard truth in front of me: a single fire or candle probably meant a single person or a small family. Undoubtedly not enough to stop even the few dozen ghouls I could see as my body stared straight ahead, much less the seventy or so others out of my line of sight. Interestingly, as we walked, I got the feeling my body, as well as the other ghouls', didn't care so much about the fire ahead of us as they did about the faint, distant sounds coming from the people around it. Sounds that, until a short time ago, would have been far below my range of hearing from this far away.

Another interesting fact about victims of whatever plague reanimated me: our bodies have enough remnant human instinct to take the path of least resistance. There was a wide path, maybe six or seven feet across, going straight through the woods. Most of us were on it, the packed dirt offering little in the way of brush or twigs. The trees surrounding us were old growth, tall and widely spaced. Not much debris from those ancient fellows.

We weren't moving silently, but close enough to it that the people around the fire were in for a bad night.

*****

The walking dead, as it happens, *can* breathe, they just don't need to.

The day before, when I first woke up to my body tearing its victim apart, the fight was almost over. I was seeing it from the other side now, and even knowing I was one of the attackers, part of the overwhelming force and not a potential meal, I was scared.

The sounds coming from the other dead people were what did it. Most of them stayed quiet, but a few began to huff, working their chests like bellows. It looked like a lot of work, and the handful that did it were fresh, only dead for maybe a few months. Then they hissed and moaned, a thin and reedy sound you never hear outside of a person dying.

Hearing a death rattle in an emergency room is one thing. Being surrounded by it in the middle of the night is quite another. I didn't bother suppressing the urge to run; it would have just been a waste of energy anyway. I let the fear run its course, then took the mental equivalent of a deep breath and waited for bad things to happen.

It wasn't a long delay. Shouts went up almost as soon as the dead people around me began making their shrill little noises. That strange sense of triangulated sound washed through me again, pointing exactly to where my eyes knew the source to be. I could see them there—a group, but small—flickering in and out of view between the press of corpses between us. I heard a woman scream for someone to get in a car and a faint whimper from what I assumed was a child.

The woman's voice wasn't filled with panic, which put her above me. My own early experiences with the infected, back when I was still alive, were filled with shame.

My family and I ran at every opportunity. I shouldn’t have felt bad about that—everyone else was running too—but I did. When measured against catastrophe, I came up short. There was no fight in me. I spent my life behind a desk, avoiding trouble. Nothing in it had prepared me for life-and-death struggles.

The man in the group didn't have that problem. He and his wife must have been a damned good match, because as I heard her barking orders to the rest of the group and the accompanying sound of car doors slamming, the husband (I assumed) raised an animal howl of protest. There was no trace of fear in his voice, not a shred of self-preservation. His war cry filled the night like a rock concert, shattering the silence, punctuated by a drumbeat of steel against flesh.

I saw the husband rise up against the front of the swarm, and the sight of him left me agape. He was huge, towering over the ranks of undead. The long crowbar in his hands was tiny in comparison. His swings were fast enough that the stiffened muscles in my body's neck couldn't twitch fast enough to follow them.

Fearless, the husband waded into the crowd. Strike after strike, merciless, and every one thumping into—and sometimes through—a skull. Head trauma. The only known killing blow for the thing I had become.

The sheer ferocity of the husband's attack took the swarm by surprise. It's easy to get the wrong idea when you're running away from a horde of dead people, but they're really more complex than first impressions led me to believe. As I watched, I saw subtlety in them. Rather than behaving like mindless cannibals, many of them reacted to the obvious danger by stepping back, bodies tense and cautious. Not the reaction of purely instinct-driven automatons. Closer to a predatory animal, albeit a very stupid one.

Still, the hunger burned inside me—rather, inside my body—and I was getting some of it, like a smoldering coal that could only be quenched in blood. My body didn't rush into the fray. It was clever enough to bide its time.

But it didn't run away, either.

The space between us opened for a moment, my view of the husband unobstructed. In that snapshot of time I saw his thick arms extended on the backside of a swing that took one of my cohorts off his feet, nearly decapitating him. That frozen instant showed a giant of a man with a face full of rage, teeth bared against the impossible odds. Bits of his enemy arced through the air around him, splinters of broken teeth and shards of rent flesh.

Five hundred years ago, that man could have been a Viking, a berserker unafraid as he faced an opposing force. The image of him as a barbarian from some fantasy series was only slightly marred by the jeans he wore, the polo shirt. They seemed like unimportant details, the camouflage used to hide in a modern age long since departed.

They say tragedy shows you who you really are. If I was a coward, and in fairness I have to say I was, then the husband was a hero. Laying into the swarm with nothing but rage and a length of metal to buy his family time—is there anything more deserving of the word?

The moment passed, and the swarm began to surge forward. At the same time, the car behind the man came to life, although with very little noise. If not for my body's unnaturally altered hearing, I would never have picked it up. I was confused for a moment, wondering why the engine didn't belt out the usual guttural roar, and then it dawned on me: electric car. Nearby, in the dim light, I caught the outline of a hodge-podge solar array on a crudely slapped together scaffolding. I realized I was looking at a carefully crafted and well-orchestrated escape plan.

The giant, crowbar-wielding warrior must have sensed the change in the swarm, then, because he went from reckless abandon one second to retreat in the next. The car was already moving as he turned from the dead in front of him and sprinted toward it, leaping onto the roof with enough force that I could hear his belly slap the metal. A few ghouls snatched at his feet, but the man's tree trunk legs shot like pistons into the faces of his enemies.

And then they were gone, taillights dwindling into the night.

The swarm followed them, of course. The corpses around me might not have been totally without guile, but they were far from smart. Distance didn't matter to them. Speed didn't enter into the equation. My own body was feeling such crippling waves of hunger I had a hard time remembering that eating people was a bad idea.

There was only the need, and the ability to move. That ceaseless drive forward.

The destruction left behind by the husband was impressive. A full dozen bodies lay on the ground, a few of them still twitching as their not-quite-destroyed brains attempted to operate their bodies like a child behind the wheel of a car. It was somehow sad, even having seen them attack an innocent person only a few minutes before.

The sun rose as we carried on.

EIGHT

Ethan may have had a nose for trouble, but it was Hicks who had the sharpest eyes. Walking out on point, the stringy young man held up a fist, signaling everyone to stop. He turned and motioned Ethan forward.

"What have you got?" he asked when he reached him.

"Sign," Hicks whispered, pointing. His finger indicated a tree trunk and small cluster of leafy, sickly-looking plants. Ethan didn't see anything wrong, the plants just looked like plants, but Hicks sounded convinced. "Somebody done been through here. Maybe a day or two ago, if that."

"How can you tell?"

Hicks motioned him closer to the tree and pointed at a section of bark about chest high. "You see that there light spot? Looks like a little scrape. Like somebody braced a hand on it steppin' over that poison ivy."

"That's what this shit is?"

"Yep. Don't go wipin' ya' ass with it. Look here." He squatted down and pointed at a few stalks near the edge of the cluster. "These is broke. Like somebody stepped on 'em. And there's tracks goin' off thataway. They's faint, but I can see 'em. Regular tracks though, don't look like infected. Too even."

Ethan looked, but saw only a featureless carpet of dead leaves stretching off into the gloom.

"You want me to follow 'em, boss?"

Ethan pondered it for a moment, thinking that Hicks had just spoken more in the last thirty seconds than in the last six months, and then nodded. "Might be survivors nearby. If so, we need to know their disposition."

“Right y’are.” Hicks hunched down and moved off through the woods. Ethan signaled the change of direction, and motioned for the others to maintain five-yard intervals.

The four men moved cautiously, minding where they put their feet and doing their best not to make noise. Hicks was practically a ghost, sliding easily between trees while dodging low hanging branches and sparse foliage. *Give that man a ghillie suit, and we’ve got ourselves a sniper.* Ethan resolved to mention it to Lieutenant Jonas the next time he got a chance.

Holland was only slightly less adept, moving with calm, practiced ease, eyes constantly alert. He might have been an insufferable shit at times, but Ethan couldn’t deny he was a good man to have on his side in a fight. As was Cole, for that matter.

Ethan swiveled his gaze to look at the powerful gunner. He carried an M-4 loosely in his hands, his heavy SAW dangling across his back on a makeshift sling. If the weight of the big weapon bothered him at all, he didn’t show it. He carried it as effortlessly as he might carry an empty backpack. Ethan was a strong man, but doubted he could have done the same quite so easily.

Less than half a mile from where Hicks had first spotted the trail, he stopped short again, holding up a fist. He leaned forward, peering at something in the distance, then abruptly motioned for the team to take cover. Ethan ducked to his right and slid on his belly beneath the boughs of a cedar tree. Once hidden, he crawled slowly forward and peered through his ACOG sights, making sure to stay well hidden beneath the thick, spiny branches. The modest 4x magnification on his optics allowed him to see movement topping a rise about a hundred yards ahead. As he watched, the shifting shadows resolved into a horse and rider.

The rider held a lever action rifle casually in one hand, stock resting on his thigh and the barrel pointed in the air. He was moving at a slow canter, evidently concerned with not making any unnecessary noise. A sensible precaution, considering how many infected there might be in the area.

Behind him, the figures of two more riders emerged, similarly armed and moving at the same pace.

With no time to lose, Ethan belly crawled to where he'd seen Holland duck down behind a moss-covered boulder. When he reached it, he spotted Holland's boots sticking out from the far side. He whispered the sharpshooter's name and saw his face appear over the top. Ethan kept his head down and crawled over

"Think you can move up that slope and find an elevated firing position before they reach us?" he whispered.

Holland looked up the low hill to his right, gauging. "Yeah, I think so. If Cole stays where he is, he can lay down cover fire if I'm spotted. Make sure he knows where I'm going."

"Can do."

"What about Hicks?" Holland asked.

"Not sure. He disappeared, but if I had to guess, I'd say he's doing the same thing you're about to do, but on the other side. I sure as hell hope so, anyway."

Holland nodded and moved off without another word, silently winding through the press of foliage. Ethan was glad he and his men had taken the time to apply face paint and put on digi-cam headscarves. The additional camouflage would increase their chances of avoiding detection. Full body armor and ballistic shields would have been nice as well, but all the extra weight would have slowed them down. They hadn't even bothered with helmets.

He checked the riders every few feet as he worked his way over to Cole, but they didn't give any indication of having spotted him or his men. Ethan could hear the soft clomp of hooves on the spongy ground and the creak of leather from the saddles. In just a few minutes, the riders would be in range.

"What's the plan?" Cole asked.

"Hold position here, and keep those riders covered. I'm going to go out there and get their attention. If they break bad, Holland and Hicks will light 'em up. You stay in reserve, and don't open fire unless I tell you to. Okay?"

Cole frowned, not liking being left out of the action. "All right, man. But just so you know, if you get in trouble I'm a' bust these motherfuckers up. Orders or not."

"Let's hope it doesn't come to that. Remember, you open up with that SAW and you're going to bring every infected within five miles down on our heads. Just stay cool, all right? Don't forget, we're in the fucking red out here." Ethan patted him on the arm and began working his way forward to intercept the lead rider.

Once he was in position, he was less than forty yards away from the horsemen. Keying his radio was a risk at this range, but he had to do it. "Echo, Foxtrot, how copy? Over."

Jonas' rough voice crackled in his ear. "Copy loud and clear, Foxtrot. What's your sitrep, over."

"Three possible hostiles in sight, on horseback, armed, headed toward the U-trac. They're less than forty meters in front of me, and we've got 'em surrounded, over."

"Any chance you can take them alive? Find out who they are and where they're headed? Over."

"Affirmative. Just so you know LT, if there's three, there's bound to be more. No way they'd come after the U-trac unless they brought friends with them. You might want to send out a few more patrols. Over."

"Acknowledged. Let me know how things work out. Over."

"If it goes bad, you'll know soon enough. We're less than a mile away. Over."

The radio went silent for a few seconds. Ethan could just picture Jonas' face pinching down and the colorful expletives spewing forth. If there were riders less than a mile away, then the whole platoon was probably in for a fight. "Copy, Foxtrot. Watch yourself, and get those raiders back here in one piece, over."

"Wilco. Foxtrot out."

He could see the riders clearly now. The one in front was older with gray hair, a grey beard, and a lean, craggy face. He carried a big revolver on one hip and a hunting knife on the other. The edge of a black wide-brimmed Stetson concealed his eyes as he searched the ground along the same path that Hicks had been taking. *Following the same tracks, maybe? But why in the other direction?*

The other two men were younger, but not boys by any stretch. Like most men since the Outbreak, they sported long, bushy beards and tied their shaggy hair back under headscarves. They both carried repeating rifles similar to their leader's. Their clothes looked in good repair, if stained and filthy, and they stared around searchingly, clearly on the lookout for trouble.

Something about them struck Ethan as not quite right, at least not for marauders. For starters, most raiders armed themselves with scavenged assault weapons. Why would they go after a military transport with lever action repeaters? They had to know that their weapons' slower rate of fire would be a huge disadvantage against trained soldiers armed with automatic rifles. If that was the best they could do, it was going to be a short fight indeed. Then there was the question of why they were following the tracks. If they were after the transport, why the hell were they taking the time to follow a random trail out in the middle of nowhere? It didn't make sense.

When they were finally close enough, Ethan eased his rifle around a tree and called out, "Stop right there."

The riders sat up straight and went still, nervous hands tugging at the reins. "Don't even think about trying to ride away. You're surrounded. Two snipers have you in their crosshairs, and there's a machine gun pointed at your horses. Drop your weapons, and keep your hands where I can see them."

The one in the lead lifted his head and pushed back the brim of his hat. Unlike his two companions, his face was stoic and unconcerned. "And just who the hell might you be?" he asked.

“Staff Sergeant Ethan Thompson, United States Army. And from here on out, I’ll be the one asking the questions. I told you to drop your weapons. Do it now. I won’t ask you again.”

The old man stared hard, glaring at Ethan with an unsettling, intelligent gaze. For a few tense heartbeats, Ethan thought he might try to level his weapon or spur his horse away. The men behind him looked on, clearly waiting for their leader to decide what to do. Ethan controlled his breathing, kept his aim fixed, and felt his finger begin to tighten on the trigger.

“Do as he says.”

Ethan let out a breath.

The old man tossed his rifle to the ground, then his pistol and his knife. The other riders hesitated for a moment before following suit.

“Get down from your horses, slowly. Keep your hands up. Try anything stupid and it’ll be the last thing you ever do.”

The men did as Ethan ordered, dismounting carefully and advancing with their hands over their heads. The leader’s stony, glacial expression never wavered.

“That’s far enough. Get down on your knees, put hands on your head, cross your feet, and don’t fucking move.”

Ethan gathered his legs beneath him to stand up, but before he could, Hicks emerged from the trees like an apparition. He approached the horses, let them smell his hands and nuzzle him, and then took their reins while whispering in low, comforting tones. He tethered them to a low branch, then stepped up behind the three prisoners.

“Now listen here,” he said. “I don’t wanna kill you, and y’all don’t wanna die. So let’s do this nice and friendly-like.” Quickly and efficiently, the wiry soldier bound the riders’ hands with zip ties, lashed them together with para-cord, and motioned for Holland and Cole to exit cover.

“You spot anybody else out there, Hicks?” Ethan asked.

"Nope. Just these three. Don't worry, anybody else comes around, the horses'll let us know."

Ethan opened his mouth to ask him what he was talking about, hesitated, and decided to let it go. Hicks was a strange one, but he seemed to know his business. He turned his attention back to the captives.

"Who are you, and what are you doing out here?" he asked, addressing the leader.

"My name's Zebulon Austin. Formerly of the US Marshals service, now sheriff of Fort Unity. The big fella here is my nephew Michael, and this man is Christopher Hedges, one of my deputies. We're on our way to a little trading village not far from here. Folks call it Broken Bridge. Maybe you heard of it?"

Ethan exchanged a glance with Cole and Holland. Both men shrugged, keeping their weapons pointed at the captives.

"I'm afraid not. But then again, I haven't been out this way in a long time."

"I'll tell you a town I *have* heard of," Holland chimed in. "It's called Hamlet. Don't suppose you know anything about that place, do you? We ran into some of its fine citizens on the way out here. On horseback, just like you guys. Seems like a hell of a coincidence, don't you think?"

"There's lots of folks around here got horses," Zebulon responded defensively. "And we ain't from Hamlet. Place is full o' slavers and cutthroats. Folks like us don't go there. Not unless we want to end up dead or in chains."

"All right, that's enough." Ethan cut in. "We're wasting time. If these guys are legit, there should be some record of their town back at Bragg. LT can radio for confirmation. If they're lying, he'll know what to do about it. Hicks, think you can handle those horses?"

"Yep."

"Good. Holland, take point. Cole, you're with me. Let's get moving." After helping Zebulon and his men to their feet, the group moved off north toward the U-trac and the rest of First

Platoon. Along the way, Ethan radioed an update to Lieutenant Jonas. The old soldier acknowledged, and told him to get back as quickly as he could.

Zebulon turned to Ethan. "Don't suppose you'd mind telling me what the Army-"

"No talking," Ethan said, cutting him off.

The older man's face darkened. "Now listen here-"

"Do you want to march the next mile with a fucking gag in your mouth? 'Cause that can be arranged."

"There ain't no call for you to be talking to him like that." It was the man Zebulon had identified as his nephew, Michael. He stood half a head taller than Ethan, with big, wide shoulders and a deep, booming voice. Ethan called out to Holland to hold up.

"I'm only going to say this one more time." He stepped in front of the captives and gave them his hardest stare. "No. Fucking. Talking. Open your yaps again and I'll wrap your faces with duct tape. Now move."

The men remained silent as they forged on, but their anger was palpable. Ethan felt a twinge of regret at his harsh words, but he couldn't afford to let sentiment affect his decisions. If these men were who they said they were, he could always apologize later. If not, well … it wouldn't much matter what they thought of him.

When they were about a quarter-mile away from where the U-trac had stopped, Ethan's radio came to life.

"Foxtrot, Echo. Be advised, we have incoming. Repeat, we have incoming, over."

Ethan felt his heart lurch. "Copy, Echo. Living or dead? Over."

"Dead. Very fucking dead, and lots of them. Coming at us from the east. You'd best circle around north and approach from that vector, but do it fast. If you're not here in ten minutes, stand off and find shelter for the night. Over."

"That many? Over."

"More'n enough to moat us in. Over."

"Copy, Echo. Foxtrot en route. Out."

"Trouble?" Cole asked.

"Infected. Big horde of them closing in on the U-trac. Holland, come on back here." Ethan gestured at Hicks. "Think you can get these men back to camp on horseback?"

Hicks responded by stepping up and swinging easily into the saddle like he'd done it a thousand times. For all Ethan knew, maybe he had. Zebulon frowned; Hicks was sitting on his horse. Ethan let out a breath. "Okay then. Up you go."

He and Cole helped the captives back into the saddle, two of them riding double on a big dappled mare and the last on a feisty looking Arabian. Ethan motioned for Holland to hop on behind the third hostage.

"Why me?"

"Because I'm not making Hicks lead the horses *and* watch the prisoners," Ethan replied. "Your job is the latter."

Holland frowned and muttered under his breath, but did as ordered. Once seated, he unsheathed his K-Bar and let the captive in front of him see it. "Just so you know, if you try anything…"

The man set his jaw angrily. "Understood."

"Good." Holland grinned and patted him on the shoulder. "You and me are gonna get along just fine."

Ethan turned to Hicks. "Head northeast to get around the horde, then circle back to the U-trac. We'll get there as fast as we can."

Hicks nodded once, then flicked the reins and turned his mount. The horse set off at a slow gallop, the others following behind on their tethers. Soon, they were out of sight, the sound of hooves beating against dirt fading into the darkening forest.

"Looks like it's just you and me again, Isaac."

The big man grinned and switched weapons, sliding the M-4 around to his back and giving his SAW a quick, practiced check. “Just like Singletary Lake.”

Ethan grimaced. “Don’t fucking remind me. Let’s get moving.”

The two soldiers set off at a quick jog. They hadn’t gone ten steps when a sudden, staccato cracking sound filled the air. They glanced at each other and quickened their pace.

Gunshots.

Never a good thing.

NINE

After the first few minutes of chasing that car, I couldn't help but feel some solidarity with the many dogs of the world. My body set out after the fleeing vehicle with as much enthusiasm as your average mutt, albeit slower. But much like the endeavors of our canine friends, the pursuit was doomed to failure.

The morning was clear and sunny, the kind of day your average person wouldn't mind taking a walk in. I would have been right there with them if the horde hadn't come upon a town. For most of my time as a dead guy, I'd been walking in the woods, or at least rural areas. But a few hours after dawn, my swarm came to a little hamlet. Or maybe it was a village. Possibly both.

I joke because thinking about it too seriously only makes the whole thing worse. In the dead of night, it's easy to forget just how far we've fallen. The cloak of darkness softens all the hard edges and makes the world a place that might have just run down on its own, so long as you don't stare at it for too long. In the harsh light of day, however, the facts were impossible to ignore.

The plague came suddenly, that I remember with perfect clarity. There wasn't a lot of space between the beginning of the violence and the total dissolution of modern society. You'd think it would have been a slower process in the sleepier parts of the world, but that was exactly the problem. When it became obvious some major-league shit was tumbling down, everyone had the same thought: Go to the little places. Find somewhere out of the way. Everyone knew of some one-horse town they'd been to as a kid, or where they rented a room at a bed and breakfast.

The thing about the metropolitan majority is there were a whole fucking lot of us. Between us, we knew of virtually every place most city dwellers only rarely ventured to. The result was the rapid and cataclysmic destruction of small-town America. It happened faster than even the large cities. People had flooded places like the little town I was walking through, a sea of humanity that would have been an impossible burden even in the best of times, which these definitely were not. Everywhere I looked, bodies lay in piles.

Even though I was dead, with little movement of air through my sinuses, the stench still reached me. The image you might get is of neatly heaped corpses, just like living people, but unmoving.

No. Not that. These were old and decaying, shredded and more rot than good flesh. Bones stuck out where animals and ghouls had worried the skin and muscle away. They were steaming piles of putrid meat, liquefying in a stew that only got worse over time. Not just a few of them either. They lay in numbers beyond counting. One particularly towering example had a snowplow parked halfway through it. Some survivor had scraped the dead off the street, leaving what became a dark brown streak of blood and shit and spinal fluid and God knows what else behind.

Cars were everywhere, like old pictures of Woodstock where traffic was backed up for a dozen miles. Many of them were wrecked, the dents and crumpled metal already browning to rust. The buildings were either vandalized or unkempt, not yet as decayed as the people or even the vehicles, but still on their way to a state that could only be thought of as post-civilization.

The grass was high, weeds invading every crack and crevice. I began to realize how much effort it took for human beings to impose their will on the world now that the gears had stopped turning. Nature, the other hand, was equally (if not more) determined to have her way. Green things crept across what appeared to have been a quaint little town, reclaiming it for the earth.

If there was any better proof the world had ended, I couldn't think of it. As my swarm walked through the town, the overwhelming evidence of human suffering and tragedy reached a critical mass, like listening to music so loud that increasing the volume stops making a difference. At a certain point, the saturation reaches its maximum and you arrive at a state of rough balance. My mind couldn't turn away from what I was seeing, and forget about trying to get my body to do it for me. There was no escape.

It hurt, that walk. There is no better way to put it. I've never been the type to cry over ads on television begging me to feed the children, or adopt an abused animal. Like many, I built a careful little wall around myself that insulated me from the terrible facts of the world. Sad when you think about it, and worse when the practical application becomes clear: I was not in any way prepared for the drastic fall of humanity. There were no emotional calluses to protect me from the heat of experiencing it firsthand.

Then again, what could prepare anyone for what I was seeing? Maybe genocidal wars in far-off places, but short of that, my mind went blank at finding a comparison. I would have cried if it had been possible, or turned way. But my body, ever focused on its next dining experience, had no soft points. No emotional reaction. Just a vague disdain for the wasted food around it and the implacable urge to feed.

I tried not to think about the loss each of those wasting bodies represented. Which of them might have been the next Einstein or Lincoln? Was the child whose spine my body stepped on meant to create great art? Write the quintessential American novel as so many people have tried to do? And even if none of the poor rotting souls close by had high destinies before them, so what? Each of them was a mother, father, brother, sister, son, or daughter. From the brightest practitioner of the most arcane sciences right down to the guy who worked the grill at my local burger joint, they were all human beings. Dreams and hopes and plans all wrapped up in a fragile body with infinite potential before them.

How huge a tragedy was it that so many people died like animals in the street? Pretty fucking enormous, to me at least.

Walking through the dead streets of a dead town that was only a slim fraction of a dead county in a dead state that comprised one fiftieth of a dead country in a dead world, I was hit with the realization that it was well and truly over for civilization.

There was a chance we could come back from this if enough people survived to start again. I knew that. No matter how slim or weak, the possibility existed. But the fabric of what we'd been was gone. There was no going back, not ever. My generation and maybe that of my children would remember a world that could never exist again. No matter what came after, all of history no longer mattered. It was a clean slate or nothing.

Locked inside my head, I wept. My body did not care.

*****

Long hours later, my body decided to have a rest. I don't know if it was from a lack of food or due to some other factor I was ignorant of, but I didn't question it. My muscles were no longer my own, my every movement the result of a nervous system not beholden to my whims, and the stillness gave me the illusion of control. If I wasn't walking somewhere, I could pretend it was my urge to die driving me to stand motionless.

I know self-delusion is unhealthy, but let's be real. Long-term considerations no longer applied to me.

For a while, I just enjoyed the day. Piercing sun, a sky more blue than any other I could recall—though I admit it might have been the idea that this day could be my last giving me that impression—and a breeze strong enough that even my dull senses could appreciate it.

Truth be told, I would have been thankful if a volcano had erupted a hundred yards away. Seeing the dead in that little town and knowing my future wasn't much different created some perspective. Living like this forever was something my mind just wasn't equipped to handle.

Knowing your days are short is awful, even if those days are spent trapped in the body of a nearly mindless killing machine. But worse, much worse, is the possibility you'll stay stuck that way. Because we humans are hopeless fools, I'm an optimist. Death was my only hope, but my determination to meet it only added to the sweetness of every moment between all the horrors. The town was enough to sour me on the idea of soldiering on, however small the urge had been. Having set my mind on reaching the finish line, I couldn't help squeezing every drop of life and meaning from even the dullest moments.

Hell of a time to become sentimental.

The rest of the swarm stopped with us, which took my illusions and twisted them up nicely before setting them on fire. Daylight was not kind to them, and as we stood in the middle of nowhere for no reason I could fathom, I saw what pitiful things those bodies had become.

Their flesh was withering, the pallor of death too obvious to ignore. Many carried wounds all the worse for being free of blood and gore, dry testaments to our unnatural state. Less poetic, some of those ghouls lacked limbs, faces, and in one case, most of their midsection. Horrible to see, worse to think about, and ultimately as unavoidable as every other sight was for me.

Distant gunshots sounded again, a rapid double tap splitting the air a good distance away. The spacing of the shots rang a bell somewhere, and after a moment perusing my recent memories, I realized I'd heard them before. The very first night after the clatter of many guns dwindled down, there were those two shots, exactly those. The memory was crisp for me, solid and clear. They were nearly identical in volume, texture, and timing.

Were we chasing someone? Dim moments began to creep up on me. Those times when my awareness had been taken up entirely by the horrors around me, but my body went right on recording. I focused, and the recollections cleared enough for me to recognize it again, buried beneath my own remembered screams.

Those same damn shots.

The swarm lurched into action immediately, moving as one. My body's three-dimensional hearing propelled it toward the sound, stoking the flames of its hunger. Intent as I was on the situation, I noticed for the first time all the strange signals I had taken for background noise. The constant hum of sensory data I'd been taking as interference between my active mind and my body.

Now that I was looking for it, I knew it was anything but static. I felt my senses sharpen a little and realized they'd done so to a much larger degree the night before. I hadn't understood what was happening then—maybe it was lack of context, or maybe I wasn't wired to interpret it correctly—but my body didn't have that failing. I sifted through the input, analyzing and cataloguing, trying to better understand what my body was doing, but failed to discern anything enlightening. Finally, after hours of frustration, I turned my attention back to the matter at hand.

The repetition of those gunshots seemed odd to me. As the miles passed beneath my feet, I wondered if the whole thing was just me trying to make sense of a senseless situation. Then, around noon, I heard them again. Still far away but clear as a bell, a repeat performance that realigned the swarm in a new direction.

Odd.

TEN

Two things happened at once.

A raider darted by on a black horse, and Ethan saw the outer edge of a horde heading toward the U-trac. It wasn't a terribly large one, maybe only a few hundred strong, but it was big enough to be a problem.

"Do you think he saw us?" Cole asked. The two of them had slid to a halt when the horse and rider flashed by less than twenty yards ahead.

"Don't think so," Ethan replied. "Seems a little preoccupied."

The raider was circling along the edge of the horde, shouting and gesturing, trying to direct the ghouls' attention toward the tracks. He got too close to one of the infected and had to fend it off with a boot to the face.

Ethan didn't need to think about what to do next.

He leveled his rifle, led the rider a little bit, and squeezed the trigger. A three-round burst rattled out, muffled by the suppressor, and struck the raider high in the chest. He screamed in agony and pitched sideways out of his saddle, right into the waiting arms of the infected. The horse whinnied in fear and bolted away. As Ethan watched, the ghouls began to tear into the doomed marauder. Several of them seized him by the arms while others chomped away at his neck, shoulders, and chest. One of them buried its face in his abdomen, leaned back with a mouthful of bleeding flesh, swallowed it, and then went back for seconds. When its face came up again, its teeth were trailing a loop of pinkish-white intestine. The screams were ear splitting.

"Man, that is just wrong," said Cole.

Ethan swallowed and tugged on the gunner's arm. "Come on, let's try to get around them. Keep your eyes peeled for more riders."

Changing direction, they headed due north. As they ran, Ethan kept thinking about the raider he'd just shot. Not only his gruesome death, but the fact that he was guiding a horde. Which meant there must be other raiders out there preparing for an attack. How many there were, or where they had managed to acquire a horde of walkers, was anybody's guess. But if he and Cole could get to the U-trac first and give warning, the marauders wouldn't stand a chance.

Despite the cold, both men were sweating and tired by the time they emerged into the tall grass bordering the railroad tracks. In the distance, Ethan could just make out the shape of the U-trac. He heard the crack of gunfire beating the air like a drum, louder than before.

"Come on, man, we're almost there." He clapped Cole on the shoulder. The big man blew out a breath.

"Goddamn, I hate running."

"So do I, but it beats the alternative."

"Walking?"

"No. Dying."

Ethan set the pace as they took off again. A lookout spotted them a hundred yards from the U-trac, ordered them to stop, and called out a standard challenge. When they replied with the appropriate password, the sentry waved them in.

Lieutenant Jonas stood with his back turned peering through a pair of field glasses. When they reached him, Ethan and Cole stopped and leaned over with their hands on their knees, trying to catch their breath. Nearby, Hicks and Holland were ushering the three prisoners into a passenger car and locking them in. Only a few other soldiers were visible.

"LT, we got trouble."

"Tell me about it." Jonas lowered his field glasses and held them out. Ethan raised them to his eyes and saw a line of riflemen a hundred yards away, one rank kneeling, the other standing and firing just like they'd drilled back at Fort Bragg. Beyond them was a multitude of ragged, staggering figures teeming through the tall grass, far more than the small horde he'd stumbled upon a few minutes ago. He gave the glasses back to Jonas.

"I'm afraid that's not all of them, sir. We spotted another horde about a quarter mile that way." He raised a hand and pointed southeast. "Marauder was leading them on horseback. They're headed right for us. We should get everybody on the U-trac and get out of here."

Jonas glanced at him, his expression disappointed. "Negative, Sergeant. I want you to think real hard and tell me why that's a bad idea."

Ethan glared in confusion, biting down on a sharp retort. Instead of arguing, he stood up straight, took a deep breath, and forced his thoughts into order.

The first thing he needed to figure out was the marauders' plan. They were sending infected out ahead of them. *Why? A distraction? What good would that do?* They had to know from their first encounter that the U-trac was armored. If the marauders wanted loot, they would have to get up close and personal and find a way to get the soldiers out of their ...

"Shit," he said, succinctly.

"Shit is right." Jonas had a small smile.

"They want us to run. That's what the horde is for, to push us into a trap."

The lieutenant nodded. "What do they have that we don't?"

"Time," Ethan replied. "They don't have to kill us, they just have to disable the U-trac. Then they can sic the infected on us and keep us penned up in the cars until we run out of water. After that, we either try to escape, in which case they can pick us off at their leisure, or we die of dehydration and they get our shit without a fight."

"All in all, not a bad plan," Jonas said. "That's exactly why we're going stay right where we are."

"I assume you have a plan of your own, sir?"

The old soldier grinned. "Don't I always? Come on, kids."

Jonas walked over to a cargo container and unlocked one of its side panels. Inside was a stack of inch-thick armor coverings for the passenger cars' windows, complete with pre-installed hinges and locks. Normally, the soldiers preferred to ride without them because they obstructed airflow, rattled in their hinges, and made a hell of a racket, none of which was helpful when traveling through infected territory. Since passing Hamlet, however, the infected were not the worst of their problems.

As a precaution, Jonas ordered Holland and Hicks to grab a few people and start putting the armored shutters in place. If they had to bug out, Jonas wanted his men as protected as possible.

Looking inside the cars, Ethan didn't see any soldiers within, just the three prisoners they captured earlier. "Hey LT, where is everybody?"

"Some of them are out dealing with the horde, just enough to make it look like we have a full complement. I split the rest into two fire teams and deployed them in the woods a hundred meters out. The rest of your squad is with Schmidt up on the northeast corner. Ashman and three of his boys are set up on the other side to the west. You, me, and the rest of these apes are going to hang around and draw the bad guys in."

Ethan's stomach dropped. "Sounds like fun."

"It needs doing," Jonas said. "I don't want these fuckers dogging our trail all the way to Tennessee."

Finished with securing the prisoners and tethering the captured horses, Hicks and Holland wandered over to where Ethan stood with Cole and the lieutenant.

"Oh good, you're just in time," Jonas said, breaking a smile. "Staff Sergeant, you and these men go help Sergeant Kelly clean up the Rot. Keep an eye out for raiders while you're at it, and try not to waste too much ammo. Command gets pissy when I have to call in a supply drop."

Ethan nodded. "Yes sir." He turned to his troops. "All right, you heard the man. Let's grab some ammo and get moving."

He stopped by the armory—which was just a small freight car packed to the brim with rifles and boxes of ammo—and had each man grab a bandolier of pre-loaded thirty round magazines. Ten mags per bandolier gave each soldier three-hundred rounds, which they would be responsible for reloading once the fighting was done. Assuming they were still alive, of course.

When they reached the action, Sergeant Kelly was walking the ranks with a pair of field glasses in one hand and a stepladder in the other. Occasionally he would put the ladder down, climb it, survey the horde, and then reposition shooters to one flank or the other. Ethan was glad Kelly was the one in charge. He had a knack for keeping soldiers calm in the face of the moaning, gnashing, stomach-turning horror that was the undead.

It was a waking nightmare facing those things. Sometimes there were hundreds of them, or even thousands, marching implacably forward, their hungry eyes fixed fixated on you, teeth bared, moans filling the air, stench making you retch, fear clawing at your brain, heart hammering in your ears, instincts screaming for you to *run, run, run*. An enemy that couldn't be reasoned with, placated, or even intimidated, no matter how many of them you killed. They just kept coming, no hesitation, no mercy, relentless. They never got tired, never got discouraged. They came on like rain, like a hurricane wind, like an avalanche bent on grinding down everything in its path. A force of nature with but one unswayable goal: to feed.

Facing that, it was easy to be scared. How do you beat an enemy that doesn't care if it dies?

Ethan had asked that question, once. He had just been thinking out loud, didn't know anyone could hear him. But Lieutenant Jonas had. He'd been standing right behind him. He had chuckled, and patted Ethan on the shoulder.

"It's easy, son," he said. "You aim your gun, and you shoot one of 'em in the head. When it goes down, you pick another and you shoot it too. Keep at it until they're all dead."

"What happens if you run out of ammo?"

The old man grinned. "You got an axe, don't you?"

Even then, all joking aside, Ethan had known it wasn't that easy. The bigger the horde, the harder they were to fight. Doing so required sufficient resources, disciplined, well-trained troops, and most importantly, skilled, confident leadership. Kelly fit that bill, as did Lieutenant Jonas. But there had been a time, back when Ethan was with a different platoon, when the leadership element had failed. When one pigheaded, irresponsible idiot ignored the advice of his NCOs and made a series of bad decisions that left his men alone, low on ammo, and facing a horde nearly five-thousand strong.

What ensued was a slaughter with the bravest, most stalwart fighters being the first to die. A shit reward for having the courage to stand their ground.

He wasn't proud of it, but Ethan had been one of the soldiers running while others stayed behind. It became obvious their position was about to be overrun, and like most of the other men in his platoon, he had fled. He would have died that day if not for Cole and his ever-present SAW, and his own skill with an axe.

The memory brought on an involuntary shudder and an old, familiar anger. At himself for being a coward, mostly. But also at the idiot butterbar who, through a combination of ineptitude, inexperience, and stubbornness, had marched them headlong into disaster. *If only he'd listened to his platoon sergeant, the stupid bastard. Sixty-three men might still be alive.*

Singletary Lake. What a fucking disaster.

Kelly, however, was doing things properly. The front rank was firing from a seated position, a pair of crossed sticks propping up the forearm of each man's rifle. Behind them stood another rank with their rifles resting on Y-shaped poles to help steady their aim. There were eighteen men, all of them firing with steady, metronome cadence. A few runners moved up and down the ranks making sure everyone had ammo while also carrying spare rifles to hand out if someone got a jam. Kelly didn't want soldiers wasting time clearing a fouled weapon. Better to simply hand it off to a runner, grab another one, and get back to work.

Looking out past the front rank, Ethan could see the bodies starting to pile up in a heaping, stinking berm. A shitpile, they called it. An apt term, if not terribly imaginative. In the case of the infected, shitpiles were a good thing. They formed a barrier that slowed the walkers down by forcing them to crawl over a mound of their own permanently dead brethren. A shitpile was also a good gauge of how well a squad leader was dealing with a horde.

A nice, even line running from one edge of a horde to another indicated good management. The soldiers were calm, picking their shots carefully, and waiting until their targets were at a predetermined standoff range before firing. A loose, ragged shitpile indicated a lack of communication and discipline. It meant the soldiers were nervous, they weren't aiming properly, and they weren't paying attention to where the bodies were falling. All very bad things. The trick to beating a horde, after all, was slowing them down. A loose shitpile wouldn't slow down anything. You had to keep it precise, and that was exactly what Kelly and his men were doing.

"Heard you could use a few extra rifles!" Ethan called out over the cacophony of gunfire. "Where do you want us?"

Kelly pointed and raised his voice. "Goddamn walkers are starting to bunch up behind the shitpile. This hill keeps pushing them down to our left side. Position your men there at three-yard intervals and ten-yard vectors, but swing back in a curve with the last man ninety degrees to the front rank. Maintain standoff at thirty yards, and for God's sake, don't let 'em get behind us."

Ethan gave a thumbs-up, repeated the orders to his men, and then gestured them into motion. They took up position where Kelly requested, swinging their line backward until the last firing vector was perpendicular to the front rank. A runner came over and handed them all a pole to steady their rifles on, made sure they had plenty of ammo, and then scurried off.

Just as Kelly predicted, the walkers were slowly pushing their way to the end of the shitpile and coming up the left flank from the bottom of the hill. Ethan set his feet, adjusted his rifle against his shoulder, and sighted in. He kept both eyes open, one focused and peering through his ACOG, and the other unfocused, using it like a motion detector to keep the broader battlefield in sight.

Several infected stumbled into each other, heaving and thrashing, ruined mouths open and teeth bared. A couple of them fell down, and the ones behind them, uncaring and oblivious, stepped right over them. One of the fallen walkers began to pick its head up only to have a ragged foot smash it back to the ground. Ethan might have found it funny, if not for the fact that the downed walker couldn't have been a day over thirteen when she died. As she struggled to rise, he put the reticle just below her nose and pulled the trigger. The back of her head exploded gore on a passing ghoul's feet.

As usual, Ethan felt a wave of pity. A sense of loss at what that poor little girl might have become. At the cruelty of a God who let such things come to pass. But then he shoved it down, bottled it up, and stuffed it firmly into the back of his mind. *No time for that. Not here, not now.*

He had work to do.

He kept firing until one magazine was empty. Reloaded. Began firing again. The infected kept coming. Sometimes he got them on the first shot, sometimes he didn't, but he kept them more or less at the thirty-yard standoff. Time went by, he wasn't sure how long. His ears began to hurt from the report of so many firearms. *Should have grabbed some earplugs, idiot.* The horde switched direction, moving away from the right flank and flowing down the hill like water. They bunched, and bulged, and struggled, each vying to be the next one over the mound. Kelly moved ten men from the right flank to the left, ordered Ethan's team to move up and straighten out the front rank, and then sent a four-man fire team halfway up the adjoining hill. Now they had the horde hemmed in, trapped behind a growing hill of corpses. Caught in the saddle of two hills, the shitpile began to resemble a dam, stopping the flow of undead under its own weight. Ethan had to admire Kelly's strategy. *Force them into a hollow and pile 'em up. Clever. Gotta remember that one.*

"Come on boys, we got 'em trapped!" Kelly shouted. "Pour it on!"

Everyone was standing now. Ethan felt his face stretch into a smile but kept his breathing steady. His rifle bucked against his shoulder, over and over again. He could feel the heat of the barrel through the shroud. They were winning. They had held the line, and the undead were dwindling, a dozen or more joining the shitpile every second. He fired, and fired, and fired again, feeling a little thrill of elation every time a walker fell. Kelly goaded them on, shouting encouragement. Ethan's eyes widened, taking in the scene, searching for his next target. The hill on the right seemed to have run dry, so he shifted left. That vector was covered; he would only be creating a crossfire by shooting that way. Kelly noticed at the same time he did.

"Thompson, you and your men stand down. Wallace, have your squad fall back. Alpha can handle the rest."

Nice of you to let your own squad finish the job. Ethan shook his head, but let it go. The horde was done for and that was what counted. Let Kelly have his fun. He'd earned it.

No longer focused on his sights, Ethan could see the firing line formed a V-shape across the two hills where they had trapped the infected. The creeping unease he had felt earlier in the day came back in a rush, wiping the smile from his face.

The horde.

They hadn't come alone, and all eyes were focused down the hill away from the U-trac. No one was watching their back. In the space of one heartbeat, it occurred to Ethan they were awfully vulnerable.

In the space of the next, he heard the pounding of hooves.

ELEVEN

I winced inwardly as my teeth cracked through the bones of the teenager's fingertips.

The reaction was born of two kinds of sympathy. One for the unavoidable loss of life to the bottomless hunger within me, and the other out of shared agony—I lost fingers the same way. There was no pain for me now, but I remembered what it was like having a chunk of my hand bitten off. And I'll be damned if at times it didn't feel like those digits were still there.

The boy's scream was deeper than I would have expected, and he struggled hard. Give credit where it's due, the kid didn't go down without a fight.

Unfortunately for him, he was outnumbered by a wide margin. The small camp my horde came across held only half a dozen people in it, him the last one living. The afternoon sun filtered through the trees, carefully placed and manicured in the little park we were in, dancing from the leaves to dapple across the boy's face.

Then another ghoul tore away his cheek while a third plunged its fingers into the soft meat of his gut, and his story was done.

Everyone ends the same way. We die and entropy takes hold, our bodies disintegrating into a million little pieces. What I—my body, rather—was doing didn't seem all that different. Just faster. Before long, what had been a boy was only a red smear outlined by hair and the odd bone that hadn't been dragged away.

I felt the blood dripping down my face and tried to wipe it off on my sleeve, but as always, my arm didn't respond. It irritated me that I was unable to even do that much. I couldn't even be a *neat* murderer.

It's the little things.

The camp was trampled beneath the weight of our swarm, tents flattened and supplies crushed. More gunshots had peppered the air during the long day, the last set leading us directly here. A deep suspicion took root in me, one I tried my best to ignore. It was outlandish to the extreme. After all, who could be that evil?

It seemed impossible that someone would lead us here on purpose.

And really, there was every chance the deaths of the teenagers camping here was just the misfortune of kids living in a world that had become a horror movie turned real. A small, sardonic part of me noted that they shouldn't have set themselves up this way. There are reasons the stereotypes exist.

Giving myself a mental shake I threw off that thought. Jesus, I had spent too much time dwelling on my situation. It was leading my thoughts to dark places. Though as a practical matter, they really shouldn't have been camping in flimsy tents with no weapons right next to a road. Might as well have been hanging steaks around their necks.

The camp was small, though. I had no doubt someone was herding us toward a destination, but they could have easily missed the poor kids here. The tents were covered fairly well, hidden beneath debris and boughs to camouflage them. There had been a fire but someone had smothered it with dirt. If my body hadn't walked right into it, I might not have even noticed.

As the swarm left the trampled campsite behind, civilization happened. It wasn't a gradual process; one minute our feet were scraping along the blacktop of that dusty country road, the next we were coming around a bend in sight of buildings. Bigger than the small towns behind us, but not a city by any stretch. Buildings that stood more than two stories high, chain restaurants and stores poking out among the faded old brick.

Wherever we were, it wasn't small. A medium-sized town but just as empty of life as anywhere else.

Well, that's what I thought.

*****

Our movement through the city was a sort of paradox. It was much slower going than the forest, but infinitely more interesting. I'm not hating on nature or anything, but after a while, the trees tend to blur together.

Night had fallen, but the moon was near full and bright, transforming the city into a washed-out ghost of itself. I felt as if I were in an old photograph, a faded likeness of what used to be.

The swarm worked its way through the labyrinth of broken streets, shattered glass crunching underfoot. On several occasions, we came across completely blocked streets and turned around only to wend our way to another.

During the long trek from barrier to barrier, I worked on sifting through the things my senses were telling me. I was paying attention well enough this time that as the sun set and the world went black, I felt the gradual sharpening of my perceptions. Imagine suddenly being able to tell scents apart like a dog, to hear like an owl, for the sensitivity of your skin to raise up so high that the brush of a single hair feels like a finger touching you.

My senses didn't go quite that far, not individually. But as I took in new smells and sounds, and felt every tiny wisp of air, the individual parts added up. It was a lot of noise to work through, but I gritted my teeth, so to speak, and did it.

My vision didn't get any better, but it became obvious the strange disassociation I'd felt a few days before hadn't been because my body was less sensitive. Rather, my mind had been too distracted and set in its ways to understand what was happening.

Over the course of a few hours, punctuated by another pair of gunshots, I brought myself into a rough harmony with all the input. And man, let me tell you, I kind of wish I hadn't.

My chest rose in tiny breaths, not enough to see with the naked eye but more than sufficient to bring a host of smells to life. There was the stench of my body as it slowly desiccated, the fading smell of piss and shit leftover from my victims' final evacuations as they died. When I tell you that was the least of it, it's to make you understand the sheer volume of awful that came with my efforts.

There were bodies decomposing somewhere in the city. Nearly every surface was streaked with old blood. Streets, walls, cars, you name it. The iron scent of it turned up the volume on my body's hunger, and as we passed carefully erected barricades, I realized this place had been staged for a battle. I'm not a military guy by any means, but even to my untrained eye, it was obvious people had made a stand here.

And they lost.

My theory was borne out as we made it deeper into the town. The place was like a giant blood droplet hitting the ground—the outskirts were spattered with it but the closer to the center you got, the thicker the coat.

We entered a sort of bailey, an open killing ground running the length of the street, which stopped abruptly at a tangled wall of old vehicles. The spaces between buildings on either side were stuffed solid with waste and debris, and the ground … it was like a paint truck had jackknifed there. I never knew there were so many shades of blood. The pavement before me was brown with it, and black, and maroon, and even the bright crimson of fresh arterial flow. There were shoe prints, boot tracks, and even the outline of bare feet in a dozen shapes and sizes, with and without whole sets of toes.

It reminded me of those old dance mats, you know? The ones with the outlines of feet and dotted lines to show you how to move.

The wall of cars fifty yards ahead of us wasn't any cleaner. Indeed, from what I could see, it was worse. Jagged pieces of metal jutted out all over, lumps of flesh with dangling trailers of skin adorning them. The wall stretched wide to rest against the ground floor of an old church on one side, turn-of-the-century stonework making the twisted steel seem weak. On the other, the wall blended into the facade of a coffee shop, one of those international chain deals with shitty coffee but great atmosphere.

A thin cry drifted over the barrier in front of us, and the entire swarm perked up as one. A few seconds later, a grating shuffle reached my ears coming from our far left. As we moved toward the wall of cars, excitement rose up within me. This was an obvious trap, and the odds looked good that I was about to die. To be set free.

Right then, the piles of trash and debris in one of the blocked-off alleys burst apart, revealing another swarm of undead.

Then all hell broke loose.

Our combined numbers surged against the line of abandoned vehicles, pushing like a colony of ants against a massive piece of food. I saw other cars behind the line acting as braces to keep the whole wall from collapsing under the strain.

There must have been enough attacks that the defenses had been badly tested, though, because to my right I saw one of the cars start to move, giving a low squeal as the tires fought against the bloodied pavement. The bracing vehicle behind it was perpendicular and off by a few degrees, which was enough to allow the horde to shove its way through. A narrow crack, just a person wide, but when a dam begins to crumble you don't think, *oh, it's just one little hole*. You see that jet of water bursting through, and you understand it's enough. The game is over.

We poured into the gap and across a cleaner section of town. There were signs of recent habitation: the smell of old, doused fires, a scattering of empty cans of food, even what I was sure was a bucket used as a toilet. Not a large area behind the wall, but one that was marked by human habitation.

My body moved with the rest of the swarm, following our perfect directional sense toward the sound of that shout. It was forward of the small guard area—I was assuming its function, but it seemed reasonable—but not far off. A block down the road from the barrier might as well have been a different world altogether.

The streets were clean, free of the crumbling remains of society's fall. No glass or dead to be seen, but signs of living people everywhere. Clothes strung across wires between buildings, the smell of food cooked not long before, a hundred little things that raised my spirits with the hope that people could carry on and then crushed them as I realized my swarm was inside their defenses. A wailing cry broke out so close to us that it seemed to come from within our ranks.

My eyes were dragged toward a building, heavily fortified with armored windows and spiked defenses. Another wail, and the swarm surged toward it in a wave. For the briefest moment, I thought the people inside would have a chance. The place was clearly a fallback point, and more than sufficient to hold off a bunch of dead bodies. That hope died a sad and quick death, though. The people inside must have been in a rush, and who could blame them when two large swarms of ghouls appeared in silence in the middle of the night?

Circumstances can change even the most innocuous mistakes. Leaving a door open used to be a small sin.

Now it was a fatal one.

For a brief moment, a small candle of hope burned within me that this was some kind of trap. Immediately inside the door was a narrow stairwell, the doors on either side of the landing boarded over. The only direction to go was up.

It seemed a perfect killing zone to me, and I couldn't get the image of cows herded down a slaughter chute out of my head. I was somewhere in the middle of the crowd bustling into the building, the stairs rapidly filling with the dense press of the walking dead. Ahead I saw the narrow stairway bristle with them, and my heart leapt as the overwhelming thunder of gunfire pounded against my eardrums.

Boom, boom, boom, boom, boom, boom. Click. Click.

“Shit, I'm empty,” a voice shouted, blowing out my candle of hope. “Get out the window and head across the roof!”

Hearing human speech rocked me. It shouldn't have, since I'd spent my entire life not thinking twice about people talking. But while I had my thoughts to keep me company, they weren't words. People so rarely think in language. It's just too slow.

Days of hearing nothing but moans, screams, and breathy rasps left me unprepared for the casual utterance of structured language. It was a sudden reorientation toward the real world. It was only then that I understood the drift happening to me: the world and the horrible things in it had slowly become less and less real to me.

A lance of pity pierced my heart. I hoped the man staying behind to buy his people time would change his mind. There were obviously too many ghouls for any one person to handle, and packed tight as we were, something as simple as a piece of furniture thrown against the crowd trying to top the stairs would be enough to buy him time.

Chips of bone and shreds of rotten flesh spattered down the stairs and across my face as the man defended his home. He cursed and shouted and—strange to my ears even more than hearing speech again—laughed as he pumped away in tight swings with his crowbar. It wasn't the kind of laugh that sends chills down your spine. There was no malice in it, no sinister urge. It was the pure, joyful guffaw of a man drinking in every last second of life. Like some Zen priest recognizing that each moment of existence is a gift.

And yeah, it was a little crazy too.

His fall was inevitable, and like the cliché, he went down swinging. As the horde tore him apart, he became another one of the endless masses of victims. Another screaming, dying voice rallying against a brutal end.

By then the front ranks were thin and my body was able to move forward enough to claw a few handfuls of meat, greedily shoving the prize into my mouth. The salty taste of hot flesh would have been easier to deal with if my brain wasn't sending signals to vomit that were being ignored.

The bodies behind me moved around the press, eager to follow the scent of the other victims. Somewhat relieved and still chewing my meal, I found myself following them.

No. Not *myself*, goddammit. My body. My body followed them.

A tall window opened into the night, the glass long since removed and the space turned into a clever escape route. The heavy wood planking over the empty hole lowered down like a drawbridge on heavy cable, landing on a makeshift catwalk that led to the adjacent building. Beyond it, the family that had escaped the swarm was trapped.

On the street below, a few dozen ghouls clawed at the brick, hands sweeping only a few feet from the isolated stretch of roof where the family cowered. A woman, eyes fierce if understandably forlorn, two adolescent children, and a baby not old enough to walk.

The older kids were boys for whom shaving was still an abstract concept. They might have been twins; each had similar hair and eyes, shape of face and bearing. The baseball bats cocked over their shoulders even rested at the same grim angle. A dozen other dead people went down the ramp to the rooftop in front of us, the family ready in the dead-end corner created by the makeshift construction behind them.

The boys were vicious and effective, knocking the first few enemies from the slender ramp easily. But they were also reckless, overreaching and allowing themselves to be grabbed. The bottom dropped out of my stomach as I watched them tumble to the pavement below under the iron grip of ghouls who got in just close enough. The woman, who I assume was their mother, screamed with such force I actually heard her voice break. Something in her throat snapped under the incoherent wail of anguish. Moments later, the horde was on her.

The best that can be said of her suffering was that it was short-lived. I'm not even going to think about what happened to the baby.

It was over fast in real time but took forever in my head. Human bodies hold so much damn blood. I was soaked in it by the end. A dark corner of my brain laughed as my body and the other monsters tried to find their way back off the roof, a process of pinball-like trial and error that took much longer than the killing.

The rest of me retreated. Turns out that while sleep was denied to me in my deathless state, good old-fashioned fugue states were still possible. I withdrew, a buffer of mental static wrapping around me like a warm blanket, and the world became a buzzing annoyance instead of an in-your-face horror show impossible to ignore.

Without that defensive reaction, I would have gone insane. I'm still not sure I didn't.

TWELVE

There were sixteen of them, split into two groups, riding in from either side of the tracks.

They had caught Ethan's platoon unawares, hemmed in, and sandwiched in the saddle of two hills, still preoccupied with engaging the undead. Their plan was obvious: ride in like a hammer and crush the soldiers against the anvil of the horde. It was a good plan, well thought out, and well executed. Well timed, even. If Kelly hadn't told Ethan to fall back, he never would have seen them coming. But as it turned out, he did.

Luck. What a lady.

Ethan watched the marauders come out of the trees and spur their horses to a gallop. For a few seconds, they stayed close to the treeline. But as they neared the bottom of the hill, one group slowed and let the other ride ahead. They realigned single-file, quickly and with expert precision, on a vector that would allow them to strafe the platoon with impunity.

Ethan called out a warning to the men behind him, and like the disciplined professionals they were, the other squad leaders echoed his command. With nowhere to run, and no cover, each man fell down onto his belly to reduce his target profile. He heard Kelly tell his men on the upward side of the hill to maintain their assault on the infected, ordering them not to allow the ghouls to get over the shitpile. The other squads turned toward the riders, lay prone, and aimed their rifles. In less than five seconds Cole had switched back to his SAW, deployed the bipod mounted under the barrel, and readied it to fire.

The riders came within range, stood up in their saddles, and took aim. *AK-47s. Seems like every marauder in the world has one these days.* Ethan brought up his sights and picked a target. Next to him, he felt the buffeting patter of Cole's SAW as he opened fire, the concussion blasting his face and pounding his ears. Ignoring the pain, he put his reticle just in front of a rider and squeezed the trigger. His aim was good, and he saw the man squeal in agony as the rounds tore into his stomach. Amazingly, he recovered quickly, bared his teeth, and returned fire.

His aim was off. The rounds cut the air over Ethan's head and sent up spouts of dirt behind his feet. Gritting his teeth, Ethan lowered his aim. *If you can't get the rider, take out the horse.* His thumb flipped the selector to full-auto and let fly a burst into the horse's forward flank. Although fighting the effects of tunnel vision, he still saw blood erupt from the animal's skin as the rounds struck home. To his shock, the animal faltered only a little and kept running. The rider tried to steady his aim, but his horse passed Ethan and he couldn't swivel around far enough to get a shot.

Cole let out a whoop as a burst from his SAW caught a rider full in the chest, stitched all the way up his face, and sent him tumbling from the saddle. Around Ethan, other soldiers' bullets found their targets, but as the raiders swung their mounts and rode away, only a handful of horses were now absent their riders. The other men had either gotten away with only wounds, or escaped being shot altogether. That was the problem with using rifles that fired a cartridge rated as only marginally lethal against coyotes, much less people. Quite often, even when you caught them center of mass, the bad guys lived long enough to run away, or stay on their feet for a while and keep fighting.

The raiders had taken a beating, and they knew it. They spurred their horses for everything they were worth, trying to put some distance between them and the pissed-off soldiers they had just attacked. Ethan saw movement in the treeline as the riders neared it, and he felt a grin tug across his face.

From the cover of the forest, several rifles and a SAW opened up. This time, it was the horsemen who were taken unawares. Bullets thudded into their bodies and their horses. The SAW roared in anger, wreaking havoc among the hapless enemy. Ethan watched a man's head disintegrate as a full-auto burst caught him in the face. Another was crushed beneath his mount as the animal pitched headlong into the ground at a full gallop. The horse rolled away and left the rider screaming on the ground, his hips turned sideways and both of his legs sticking out at odd angles, feet turned in the wrong direction. Ethan's smile faded.

It was over in seconds. The guns ceased their chatter as half of the now riderless horses galloped away. The other half lay on the ground near their riders, dead or dying. A few of the marauders still moved, clutching wounds and screaming and begging for help they weren't going to get. Ethan got up on one knee and cupped his hands around his mouth.

"Hold your fire!" he shouted at the trees. At least it felt like he was shouting, his ears were ringing so badly he couldn't hear his own voice. "We need a prisoner!"

The other soldiers emerged from cover, and with a surge of pride, Ethan realized it was Justin and the rest of Delta Squad. Private Clark was with them, the heavy gunner from Alpha Squad, one of Sergeant Kelly's men. *Must have sent him along as backup. Probably bitched about it, thought Kelly was taking him out of the action.* They kept their rifles leveled as they moved into the open, prepared to fire in an instant if any of the marauders tried for a weapon. The carnage was terrifying; men and horses lay scattered over a hundred-yard stretch, their bodies torn and broken. Before the Outbreak, the sight would have been enough to turn Ethan's stomach, which was saying something. He'd been an EMT in his former life, and had seen the results of many a fatal car wreck.

Here, a man lay shuddering and whimpering, trying to stuff his guts back into his stomach, blood pooling beneath him. His face was white as a sheet of paper, lips blue, eyes glazing over. Not much time left for that one. No use questioning him. Ethan swallowed his revulsion and moved on. Nearby, a horse lay writhing on the ground, screaming and tossing its head. He moved around its thrashing hooves and checked the next man. Face down, not moving, no rise or fall of the chest, several exit wounds between his shoulder blades. Ethan kicked him in the kidney. Nothing. He kicked him again, harder. Still nothing.

Next, he checked a kid who looked no older than eighteen. One of his legs was hanging on by a twist of muscle tissue, the pale white gleam of his patella jutting out of shredded flesh. The kid's eyes stared open, fixed and dilated. Ethan kept moving.

Finally, he found a live one. He'd taken a bullet in the hip and another in his elbow. Survivable wounds with the proper medical treatment, although dancing and boxing were no longer career options. Ethan leveled the barrel of his rifle—which he now realized he'd forgotten to remove the suppressor from—and pointed it at the man's left eye. He looked up, face frozen with fear.

"Hi there," Ethan said pleasantly. "Staff Sergeant Ethan Thompson, United Stated Army. Pleasure to meet you."

The man let out a breath, closed his eyes, and passed out.

*****

Lieutenant Jonas was pissed. He had screwed up royally, and he knew it.

"Didn't think they'd come at us head on like that," he muttered for the tenth time. "And in broad daylight too. Fuckers are getting ballsy."

"Don't beat yourself up, LT. None of our guys got hurt. That's what's important."

Jonas turned his hard, granite-colored eyes on Ethan. "I should have planned for the possibility. I should have sent a few men down to stay behind cover and watch your backs. Instead, I kept them all up here by the U-trac. Figured if I made it look like an easy target, the raiders might try to ride in, smash the locks, and make off with the loot while everybody's busy fighting the Rot. It was just damned blind luck that Schmidt spotted those riders and moved his fire team down the hillside. God knows how many men we would have lost if he hadn't. I should have sent them down there to begin with, and not kept them up here by the transport."

"Defending the U-trac was the logical thing to do, sir. It was a good plan."

"Yeah, except for the fact that my bluff got called and I wasn't ready for it. Damn near got you all killed. It should have occurred to me they might attack while the platoon was fighting the infected. I fucked up, Sergeant. I fucked up bad, and I can't afford to be making those kinds of mistakes. When officers fuck up, good men die."

Jonas looked miserable, angry, and ashamed all at once. Ethan tried to think of something helpful to say, but when he thought about it, he realized Jonas was right. The lieutenant *had* fucked up. But while Jonas didn't mind voicing his mistakes to himself, he didn't tolerate that kind of criticism from his men. He evaluated his soldiers, not the other way around. Ethan decided to change the subject.

"Any word on Austin and his men?"

Jonas nodded. "Kelly just got off the horn with Command. As it turns out, the PI geeks have access to a master list of all known survivor communities, and lists of their citizens. Those that gave 'em, anyway. Fort Unity is on the list. Austin's story checked out; he's the sheriff there."

A door clattered open on the U-trac and the man in question stepped out, along with his nephew and deputy. As they approached, the looks they turned on Ethan were not happy ones. He had to fight the urge to let a hand stray toward his pistol.

"I understand you're in charge here?" Austin said, addressing the Lieutenant.

"That's right. Lieutenant Clay Jonas, First Reconnaissance Expeditionary." He held out a hand. Austin stared at it for a long moment before shaking it.

"My men and I are headed to a place called Broken Bridge. Little town a few miles west of here. Maybe you've heard of it?"

Jonas thought for a few seconds, then shook his head. "Sorry, can't say as I have."

"It's a pretty large trading post. Couple hundred people living there. They're the third town to go dark in as many weeks. I'm on my way there to find out why."

"What do you mean 'went dark'?" asked Jonas.

"There's a few towns around here that managed to scrape together enough materials to generate electricity. Not much, but enough to power radio equipment. Sort of a network, you see. We all stay in touch with each other, share information, give warnings about marauders, do trade negotiations, that sort of thing. Three weeks ago, one of the towns didn't check in when they were supposed to. A few days later, we had another one go quiet. Then Broken Bridge. One or two, we might just chalk up to bad luck, but three can't be a coincidence. Something happened to those towns, and I aim to find out what it was and make sure it doesn't happen to Fort Unity."

Jonas' expression hardened. It was a long instant before he spoke. "I'm sorry to hear that, Mr. Austin. I truly am."

"Seeing as you know about it, Lieutenant, what do you plan to *do* about it?"

"I'm not sure there's much I *can* do for you. We're behind schedule as it is, and we need all the resources we have with us. We expect heavy fighting where we're going."

Austin took half a step closer, glaring. "I just told you there are people dying out there. *Dying*. People you're supposed to protect. You remember swearing an oath to do that, don't you?"

"I am well aware of my responsibilities, Mr. Austin," Jonas said flatly. "I don't need a lecture from *you* on what they entail. If you have a bone to pick with the military, do it someplace else. I don't have time for it. We've got our own problems." He pointed a finger at the cluster of dead bodies at the base of the hill, marauder and infected alike. Austin's eyes shifted that way, resting there for a while. His anger dimmed.

"Of course. I heard the Army was stretched pretty thin. Didn't realize how bad it was."

"We're all doing the best we can." Jonas turned to Ethan. "Sergeant, find Hicks and have him bring around their horses. Mr. Austin, I wish you luck. If I could go with you, I would, but this platoon is needed elsewhere."

Ethan watched the hope fade from Austin's face. He had obviously expected Jonas to offer assistance, and now it was clear that wasn't going to happen. Still, he had a point. If decent, honest people were in danger, the Army had to do something about it, even if it was inconvenient.

"Maybe there's another solution."

All eyes turned to Ethan. Jonas' expression was one of warning.

"Just hear me out, sir."

"I'm listening."

"We don't need to send the whole platoon, do we? Maybe just a few guys, like three or four. I could ask for volunteers."

Jonas thought about it. "But the platoon would have to move on. You'd be stuck out here alone with no way to catch up."

"Sure we could. FOB Harkin could send a Blackhawk. They could pick us up from anywhere in the region and drop us back at the U-trac when we're done."

Ethan had met the CO of Forward Operating Base Harkin just after the battle of Singletary Lake. He was just a pilot back then, and he had flown the chopper that rescued Ethan, Cole, and several other soldiers from the roof of a boathouse. To express his gratitude, Ethan gave the man a bottle of Ten Canes rum, a box of tampons, and a jar of instant coffee—a small fortune in trade items. Ethan was willing to bet the pilot would remember him. He said as much to Lieutenant Jonas, and watched the spark of hope in Austin's eyes begin to flare again.

"Well, if you think you can talk Colonel Lanning into helping out, I suppose it's worth a shot." Jonas said. "We can spare a few men until we get to Tennessee."

"I'll get on the horn." Ethan strode off toward the U-trac. A few minutes later, he spoke with a bored sounding private and asked him to deliver a message to his CO.

"The colonel is unavailable right now, Echo. I can take a message."

"He'll want to speak to me directly. Just tell him it's Ethan Thompson, he'll know who you're talking about."

"No offense, Sergeant, but we get requests like that all the time. You'll have to forgive me if I'm not impressed."

Ethan ground his teeth. "Listen, if he finds out I called for him, and you stonewalled me, it's going to be your ass, private." It was a stretch, a gamble, but it was all Ethan had. He just had to hope Lanning remembered him.

The private sighed. "All right, fine. I'll go knock on his door. Stand by."

A minute passed in silence. Ethan tapped his feet impatiently, half-expecting the private to come back and tell him the CO had refused to speak with him. Instead, a different voice spoke up.

"Well I'll be damned. I understand it's Staff Sergeant Thompson now, is that right?"

"Yes sir. I'm moving up in the world."

Lanning laughed. "I've been saying for years the Army's standards have gone to shit."

"Couldn't agree more." Ethan said grinning.

"To what do I owe the pleasure, Sergeant?"

"Well, for starters I wanted to find out what you did with all that swag I gave you after Singletary Lake."

"Oh man, I partied like a rock star. Me and some other pilots got sent to the Springs for some R-and-R about a week after I picked you up. Seven days, man. Seven glorious days. I drank the rum, the coffee bought me a week's food and lodging at the cleanest hotel in town, and the tampons got me three nights of the best sex I've ever had in my life. I could have died happy at the end of that week."

No wonder he remembers me. "Sounds like you had a good time."

"Never better. So tell me, Sergeant, what can I do for you? I'm guessing you didn't call just to exchange pleasantries. There something you need?"

Ethan explained the situation with Austin, and his suspicion that several small survivor communities had been destroyed. Lanning's tone was businesslike when he spoke again.

"That's not good. Especially since those towns are so close to the FOB. What can I do to help?"

"I'm going to get some volunteers and go with Austin to investigate. Once we're done, we'll need some help getting caught up with my unit."

"Can do, Sergeant. I'll arrange it personally. Anything else?"

Ethan almost said no, then thought better of it. "We may need a supply drop at some point."

"What kind of supplies?"

"Out in the shit, you never know. Maybe food, maybe medical supplies. Ammo. Could be anything."

"I can't make any promises, but I'll help if I can."

"I really appreciate it, Colonel."

"Not a problem, my friend. You watch your ass out there."

"I always do. Echo out."

He turned around to see Austin standing at the doorway. "Well?"

Ethan gave him a thumbs-up. "All set. Now I just need some volunteers."

"Already taken care of." Austin stepped aside, allowing Holland, Hicks, and Cole to appear in the doorway. It was Cole who had spoken up. "You know we gotcha back, E-dawg."

Ethan hated that nickname, but coming from Isaac, he was willing to let it go. "All right then," he said. "Get your gear together. Mr. Austin, you ready to go?"

The old man nodded, eyes looking over Ethan's soldiers, clearly not happy to be traveling with the same men who captured him less than an hour earlier. *Too bad. If he wants our help, he can fucking deal with it.*

"Good. Let's get moving."

THIRTEEN

I came out of the haze when my consciousness began to slip.

It wasn't death—whatever process keeping my personality active was too strong for that—but rather, it was like being engulfed. I felt the smothering weight of my body's base urges press down on me with the force of a mountain. In the muffled quiet of my fugue state, the weight was overwhelming.

Gathering my will, I fought against it and came up like a diver desperate for his next breath. It wasn't fear of death driving me back to full alertness, it was the fear of being self-aware while the thing keeping my body alive submerged my humanity. Bad enough my body was a merciless killing machine, I didn't want to start reveling in it as well. My brain reconnected with my eyes, and immediately it was clear what caused the avalanche of hunger in my body.

A man was dashing by just outside our swarm.

Mangy heads swiveled on creaky hinges toward the stranger, the motion similar to a school of piranha locking in on prey. It was futile, however; the man easily outpaced us. I caught glimpses of him between the bodies. Thin, tall, ragged coat floating out behind him and flapping like a sail. His hair was long and matted, nearly as dirty as the dead surrounding me. The split-second when I saw his face told me a story all on its own, a single impression but a strong one.

He looked sick. Not the way someone with the flu looks. That would have been too hard to see from a distance. The stranger was hollow-cheeked, skin stretched hard across his face and eyes sunken into pits surrounded by dark circles. His complexion was ashen, a weird mixture of deathly gray—which was common enough among us dead folks—and the yellow pallor of liver failure.

The stranger had a rifle across his back, the weapon bouncing as he loped past and ahead of us. In no time at all he dwindled to a speck, but it stopped there. My swarm moved toward him and he grew again, eventually close enough to show the impatience on his face before darting down the road another few hundred yards.

And waiting there. Again.

A cold chill swept through me, clashing with the fiery hunger in my body. It hadn't taken a huge leap to deduce my swarm was drawn by the sound of gunfire, but right in front of me was proof we were being led. I hadn't wanted to believe it no matter how much the idea squirmed in the back of my mind. After all, who would deliberately lead groups of ghoulish nightmares toward gatherings of living people? Mankind had lost the vast majority of its population, leaving every person still alive a rare and precious thing.

But the evidence couldn't be ignored. Strange as the sensation was, I found my own impulses perfectly aligned with my body. Both of us wanted this man dead.

*****

Anger faded to irritation and a general sense of dissatisfaction as the day wore on. Whatever small wisps of doubt I had held evaporated by the fourth repeat performance. The stranger enticed the swarm on, occasionally vanishing into the woods only to return thirty minutes or an hour later with a new batch of ghouls in tow.

Our numbers grew. Not by the hundreds, but every handful the man brought to the main pack made us more dangerous. More of a threat. Far away as he was, I couldn't catch his mannerisms. But given his obvious psychotic desire to do harm, I could only assume he was walking on sunshine.

That thought put the song *Walking on Sunshine* in my head, and it stayed with me. It was fucking maddening.

A short aside here: Normally when you get a song stuck in your head you can just hum it or sing it and that process sort of vents the pressure. You still have to deal with whatever annoying tune is dancing around your cerebellum, but it's manageable. As soon as the song began to play, it was like a 1970s era Led Zeppelin show. Imagine speaker stacks the size of school buses, the volume as overpowering as a jackhammer to the temple.

Eventually I pushed it down to a dull roar, but my will grew weak. Not being able to easily handle the myriad strange little things our brains do was just one more blow to absorb. The strain pulled at me.

I made myself focus on the stranger and his activities. A good twenty minutes passed as I imagined all the creative ways I'd like to murder him, both as a living man and as a shambolic corpse. Knives, vehicular homicide, evisceration, a thing involving a bag of nails and sulfuric acid, scenario after scenario. Giving myself fully to the rage kept me from going crazy.

Interesting side effect, though. That damn song ended up being the soundtrack—stuck on constant repeat—to my murderous fantasies. I was reminded of the night Sheila and I rented and watched *A Clockwork Orange* for the first time, the part where Alex assaults the woman while belting out *Singing in the Rain*. I was supposed to be the strong manly man, but Sheila—

Oh, Jesus. Her name. That was my wife's name.

Memories hit me all at once. It wasn't just the missing ones, but even the pieces I'd already recalled suddenly bloomed to full color in my mind. They ceased to be still photos and cracked old films, and burst into full high-definition across the inside of my skull. Details emerged, creating context to the rapidly expanding catalog of events surging to life.

My life. With her. Coming back to me in glorious, agonizing detail.

I was caught up in the flow of it like a starving man suddenly plopped down at a buffet. I feasted on the good and the bad alike. Anything and everything about who I was. A warmth spread in my mind as the recall continued, a contentment I hadn't realized I'd possessed in life until I finally felt its absence.

My preoccupation with the flood of memories nearly made me miss the stranger when he appeared from one of his frequent side trips. The road we traveled was overgrown and winding, but even swimming in the waters of recollection, I'd noticed the world around me in a passive way. The entire country was littered with the debris of the world that was, but it still stands out to you when you pass through an area littered with military hardware.

This fact didn't seem very important to me as I rummaged through my new memories. After all, the US military was a huge and well-populated beast, especially before the bad luck that cost me my first life and pulled me into my second. I'd seen enough abandoned gear to consider it a curiosity at best. So when the sick man leading us around like ducklings emerged from the tangle of Humvees and troop carriers with a rocket launcher, I noticed. Even as a walking corpse, that's not the sort of thing you see every day.

It wasn't long until dark, the colorful striations of sky and sun blazing above us. As the stranger led us forward, his pace slower because of his new toy, I had a brief moment of hope. Maybe he'd use it to kill the swarm. Maybe he was tired of this game.

He didn't, of course. I watched the business end of the weapon bounce around as he jogged, and another brief flash of memory hit me. It wasn't a logical process, but a recollection of a movie with the same kind of rocket launcher in it, or something similar. Some hapless soldier with no experience being told to use it on a tank.

Damn. Whatever the sick man was planning, it had to be big.

*****

Long hours later we came upon a town.

It wasn't the white picket fence, mom and pop sort of place that comes to your head when you think of a small town. The first thing I noticed from my position at the front of the pack was how relatively bright the place was. The world was a darker place without streetlights, headlights, security lights, and every other source of illumination long since gone the way of the dinosaur.

Not this place. It was far from a metropolis, but like any piece of civilization, it glowed even in the small hours of the night. Torches guttered along the wall at regular intervals, and there were even some bulbs burning. Although I was hundreds of yards out, I could see the difference in the sources of light. Some steady, some flickering. Now and then a person would pass along the wall, but not often enough.

My heart sank. As the swarm closed in, we breasted a hill, giving me a view of the place from just high enough to see most of the town.

I caught a glimpse of heavy gates at one end of a mostly ruined bridge. We were already circling past that, which made sense given how heavily fortified the gate beyond the bridge was. We moved around widely, the horde eerily quiet. The only sound was the gentle hiss of our feet against the grass.

The stranger changed direction suddenly, jetting toward what looked like the edge of a large ravine. There, he was less than a hundred yards from a second gate, which was smaller but no less heavy than the one at the bridge. I tried to work out why our pied piper thought this was the best place to strike since the swarm would have to cross the bridge to fully infiltrate the town, but I couldn't quite get there.

The stranger ran along the bank, gaining distance from the swarm even as he drew us on. When he was as close to the gate as he could get without falling into the ravine, he dropped to one knee and reached around for the rocket launcher. After fiddling with it for a few seconds in the dark, he raised it to his shoulder and fired.

The blast was enormous and painfully loud. A tremendous *crack-BANG* and a brilliant plume of fire from the back of the weapon. The warhead—I think that's what it's called anyway—hit the gate like the hammer of God, smashing it from its concrete supports and leaving it burnt and twisted on the ground. An alarm began to sound, a ringing bell, followed by others along the wall. Soon, bells echoed all throughout the town. Shouts went up in their wake, spreading like wildfire.

Blinding anger took over my mind for a few seconds, and I felt a sort of resonance from my body. Bestial as it might be, it wasn't a total fool. My body locked eyes with the stranger as we approached him. We came within twenty feet, close enough for me to see his nightmare grin of blackened and broken teeth.

So close. I wanted to hurt this man for what he was doing. For what he was making me do. I wanted to tear into his flesh every bit as much as my body did, if for different reasons.

My body and I in agreement, we rushed forward, following the stranger toward a community already losing its mind in the chaos.

*****

It made sense to me once I saw it.

The large, obvious bridge above was just a decoy, barely adequate for even one person at a time to cross. Below it, hand built but obviously sturdy, was another bridge, cleverly concealed. Hiding in the shadow of the first, the second bridge was a mass of heavy wooden slats bolted and supported with long metal joints. It was wide enough to fit a small car, and looked strong enough to hold the weight.

The swarm was thinner behind me, but still pushing. Still strong. Space opened between us as we shuffled across the bridge. The stranger moved like a snake, shooting away into the darkness. My body climbed a set of switchbacks up a steep hill, which I realized was actually the bank of a low river, and then burst through the small clearing at the bridge's terminus.

"Blow it!" I heard someone shout. "Blow it and drop the backup!"

The stranger was ready, however.

"No, don't," he shouted. "There are others coming from the northern section. Just hold here for a minute!" The stranger was moving the entire time, closing in on the poor guards trying to minimize the damage.

"Hey, who the fuck are-"

The stranger slashed the man's throat, then whipped around to knock his partner to the ground, the knife gleamed wet and red as he pushed the blade into the man's heart. Once, twice, three times and done.

My body nearly had him then, but the stranger pelted away from the large, ruined doorway before we could snatch at him. We followed, of course, senses tracking every whisper of sound. The stranger ran on, doing his best to blend in until he was right on top of someone. It was a good act, worthy of awards. The stranger wailed and screamed as the horde pursued him, only dropping the mask from his face when someone got close enough to realize he wasn't one of them.

I remember following him doggedly, my body so intent on destroying the stranger it paid little attention to the people he killed along the way. Quick slashes, precise thrusts, and bodies fell. More people dead, and all because this man wanted to watch the world burn.

The swarm that pushed at my back like a tidal wave was quick to pounce on those easy meals. Once or twice, my errant flesh nearly got distracted, its attention wavering from the stranger. The only thing keeping it on task was the difficulty of fighting off the other ghouls for those meals.

Besides, I could feel that resonance. My body wasn't capable of the higher functions, but as a predator, it recognized threats. Its wants were vague and less powerful than my own, but some part of me was getting through, reinforcing its own small urge to eliminate the enemy.

The swarm flooded across the front half of the town with depressing speed. The rest of the ghouls moved around me, hunger driving them after the scattered settlers fleeing into the night. The urge to devour was rising in my own flesh as well, and would have taken over if we hadn't looked up at just the right time.

There he was. Feet dangling from the roof of a one-story building, back sitting against a partial wall behind him. Greasy hair surged with faint orange highlights as the swarm moved toward the pile of bodies the stranger left below his perch. Rhythmic as a heartbeat, his face glowed again, and he laughed to himself.

Rage like an exploding star surged through me. My body locked onto him, ignoring the dead and dying at our feet. Our hands swept upward in a clumsy attempt to grab the stranger's foot, but the distance was too great.

He laughed again, playfully wiggling his feet as he dropped a small crystal into the pipe sticking out from his fist. The lighter glowed, his breath sharp as the smoke hit his lungs. My body didn't give up, still swiping as the stranger grinned down at us.

"Gideon," the man said to himself, surveying the carnage. "You sure know how to throw a party."

Eventually my body gave up trying to catch him, submitting to the hunger. Its feeding, for once, didn't even register to me. I had thought being trapped in my own walking corpse was the worst thing imaginable. This man—Gideon, apparently—showed me how wrong I was. He was worse by miles.

Feeding would keep my body going, terrible as it was. Gideon needed to destroy, to hurt, to burn his way across the earth. My body did things because it had to. This monster did them by choice.

For that, he was going to pay.

FOURTEEN

Ethan brought Hicks along for his tracking abilities, but as it turned out, he needn't have bothered. The broad swath of coagulated body fluids, crushed plant life, trampled detritus, and the occasional discarded body part made it obvious which way the horde had travelled. Ordinarily, they would have taken it as a warning and given the horde a wide berth, but there was just one problem.

It was headed straight for Broken Bridge.

After setting out from the U-trac, they picked up the massive trail just before sundown, and not wanting to get caught in the open after dark, took shelter for the night on the roof of a long-abandoned gas station. Zebulon's nephew, Michael, tethered the horses in a tire shop across the street and stayed the night with them. They expected to see infected wander in during the night, but surprisingly, none appeared. While convenient, Ethan found the lack of ghouls disturbing. As far in the red as they were, and as much noise as the horses made, they should have seen at least a few. Despite the calm, he got little sleep that night.

His party struck camp at first light and followed the destruction for eight miles, hoping against hope their fears would go unrealized, until finally they crested a low hill less than a kilometer away from their destination.

In the valley below, Broken Bridge was in ruins.

Zeb—as he insisted everyone call him—sat quietly astride his horse, sadness creasing the lines of his weathered face. Ethan lowered his field glasses and felt his shoulders slump. The first steady hammerings of a migraine began thumping at the base of his skull.

"See any movement down there? Anybody alive?" Zeb asked, his voice tight.

Ethan shook his head, suddenly feeling tired. "Movement, yes. Anything alive? No. I'm sorry, Zeb. Did you have friends down there?"

The old lawman's jaw twitched as he nodded. "Better go down and see if there's any survivors." He touched his heels to his horse's flanks and the animal slowly began descending the valley.

"There are still a lot of infected down there," Ethan called out.

Zeb drew a weapon from behind his saddle that looked like the mother of all meat cleavers. It had a three-foot, single-edged blade half as wide as a man's palm, a two-handed hilt wrapped in athletic tape, and a simple brass crossguard. Dark ridges, whorls, and hammer marks spiraled up the oiled steel, wide at the spine but growing close and clustered near the edge. *Folded steel. Somebody forged that by hand.*

"Feel free to stay here if you want, Sergeant. We'll catch up with you when we're through."

Ethan glared at Zeb's back, biting down a sharp reply. He turned to his men, motioning them forward. "Come on. There might be someone still alive down there."

The others frowned, but followed. As they drew closer to the town, Ethan got a better look at the materials comprising the twenty-foot wall surrounding the outpost. It was built from a random hodgepodge of railroad ties, hand-cut logs, telephone poles, masonry, wide steel plates, and crushed vehicles like the kind found in junkyards. Surrounding it was a partial secondary wall of cargo containers with breaks for the main gate and a smaller service entrance around the side. The main gate looked to be intact, save for a collection of scorch marks and bullet pocks of varying sizes, indicating the town had been attacked more than once. He wondered what level of force it would take to overrun a place so heavily fortified.

Upon reaching the shattered expanse of bridge the town was named for, it didn't look to Ethan as though the horses could make it across. The bridge—one of those ugly old concrete and steel monstrosities built back in the 1950s—had long ago been destroyed, undoubtedly by a retreating military force during the early days of the Outbreak. Since then, it had been replaced by a rickety-looking wooden span with nothing but two lightly tensioned ropes for support. It looked barely strong enough to support one person, much less a full-grown horse laden with a rider and kit.

"You gotta be fucking kidding me." Ethan heard Holland's Boston accent behind him. "Hey Zeb, you know another way across this river? 'Cause no fucking way am I walking over that bridge."

"Don't worry about it," said Zeb's deputy, Hedges. "We'll show you the way."

Branching off where the highway met the river, Ethan noticed a footpath curving down around the ravine. At first glance, it didn't look as though it led to anything except a narrow beach at the water's edge. But after looking for a moment, he saw what Hedges was talking about—another bridge.

Smaller and narrower than what had once spanned the river, it was nonetheless sufficient to support the weight of the horses, although they would have to ride single-file. The smaller bridge was built in the shadow of the larger one, lower along the embankment, and covered at the edges with camouflage nets. The span in the middle had been painted to resemble the water with remarkable attention to detail, while the edges were surrounded by a small forest of cattails. If anyone happened by and didn't know what to look for, the bridge would be easy to miss. *So the suspension bridge above is just a decoy. A trap. Clever. Makes me wonder if the main gate is really a gate at all.*

There were a few infected splashing around in the water as they crossed. The river flowing below them was low, only coming up to the walkers' waists. Upon seeing Ethan's party, they began to shamble forward, tripping and falling below the surface only to rise up with water pouring from their open mouths. *So much for refilling our canteens.*

"Hey bossman," Hicks said behind him.

Ethan turned. "Yeah?"

"Want me to kill them walkers?"

"No. They're trapped; it's not worth the ammo. Besides, we're gonna have our hands full once we get across the river."

Hicks grunted, and they moved on. Ethan stayed well back from Hedges' mount and its constantly whipping tail as they walked along. The horse was nervous, clearly not happy about being so close to the undead.

Soon enough, they crossed the water and began traversing a set of switchbacks that led up to Broken Bridge's service entrance. Above them, ragged, wheezing moans began drifting down from the top of the embankment. Ethan drew his axe from its harness and turned to his men.

"All right, guys. Hand weapons only for now. We need to conserve ammo. Hang back for a bit and let Zeb and his men clear a path, then fill in the gap and start busting heads. Wear your PPE, and don't forget to maintain intervals. And for God's sake, give Cole room to swing. I don't want to have to radio for a medevac."

The big gunner grinned as he reached a hand over his shoulder and drew his bar mace. He had purchased his massive, medieval looking weapon from a blacksmith who plied his trade near Fort Bragg. Cole's mace had cost him 200 rounds of 9mm ammunition and a case of bourbon—an exorbitant sum—but by his own admission, it had been more than worth it. When armed with his heavy three-foot weapon and given room to work, he was a human engine of destruction.

Ahead of them, Zeb reached the top of the ravine, spurred his horse, and sprang forward with a shout. His wicked blade rose and fell as he sped by a walker, splitting its head down the middle like a melon. He tore his weapon free and guided his horse toward the next target. Behind him, Hedges and Michael split up, both drawing weapons similar to Zeb's cleaver. In a few seconds, all three were out of sight over the hill, but Ethan could hear their shouts and the dull thuds of steel striking dead flesh. Ethan tied his scarf over his mouth and nose, slipped his goggles over his eyes, and looked behind him. His men had already done the same.

"Up the hill!" he shouted, his voice slightly muffled. "Time to go to work!"

They increased their pace, breaking into a jog. As they cleared the rise, they saw the three riders circling the main force of the horde, closing in toward the center in a whirl of horseflesh and steel. Around and around they rode, arms rising and falling rhythmically, each stroke smashing a walker's head and sending it tumbling to the ground. Ethan was momentarily impressed at their practiced coordination, but the feeling dimmed when he realized the horses would be useless in the close confines of the town. Picking up speed, he ran to his right, angling toward a smaller group of undead closing in from the north.

"Hicks, you're with me. Cole, you and Holland break left. Make sure Zeb doesn't get blindsided."

"You got it."

Hicks gripped his heavy, short-handled spear and followed Ethan as he ran toward the eastern wall. There, a loose knot of about a dozen undead waited for them. Slowing his pace, Ethan spun his axe around and swung the spiked end at the lead ghoul's temple. It connected with a satisfying *thunk*, making the walker go stiff for a moment before collapsing. Beside him, Hicks ducked under a walker's reaching hands and thrust his spear upward, moving with the casual grace of long practice. His weapon pierced the shallow skin under the ghoul's jaw, penetrated upward through its soft palate, and cleaved its rotten brain until the point stopped against the top of its skull. With a quick downward jerk, Hicks freed his spear and turned to look for his next victim.

The two of them kept at it, Ethan killing ghouls with wide swings of his axe, and Hicks dispatching them with quick, precise spear thrusts. Every few seconds they backed off, circled their undead assailants, picked new targets, and moved in to put them down. All the while, they kept in mind the golden rule of fighting the undead: keep moving, and don't get greedy.

As they fought, Ethan took note of the walkers' condition. The corpses were fresh, probably not dead more than a day or two. Their clothing was in relatively good shape, as were their shoes, and their wounds were still red and raw, not blackened and crusty. *Townspeople,* he thought. *The horde that killed them must have moved on.*

From the corner of his eye, Ethan saw another small horde emerge from the town's shattered service entrance and start toward the circling horsemen. Holland and Cole moved to intercept, weapons at the ready. Cole carried his heavy bar mace as if it weighed no more than a twig, while Holland, unable to wield heavy melee weapons due to his slight build, deftly spun a pair of long-handled hatchets.

When they reached the walkers, Cole began swinging his mace in a steady figure-eight pattern, each downswing cracking an infected skull like an eggshell. Slowly, he plodded along, keeping his weapon moving and leaving a trail of grisly, twice-dead corpses in his wake. Holland circled to his right, his hatchets whirling. Unlike Cole's juggernaut brute force, Holland relied on speed, disabling the walkers with fast, precise slashes to knees, ankles, and hamstrings before dispatching them with overhand blows to the backs of their necks. When other walkers got too close, he knocked them over with a display of kicks that would have made his old Tae Kwon Do instructor beam with pride.

After a grueling few minutes of fighting, Ethan and his men had eliminated the smaller hordes that wandered out of the ruined town, while Zeb and his riders had cut down the main force. Once the first wave was down, Ethan ordered his men to back off, take some water, and catch their breath. Zeb's crew followed, giving the secondary horde time to clear the gate, and giving their horses a chance to rest.

"You boys doin' all right?" Zeb asked. He was still fresh, having done his fighting from horseback. Ethan's men were winded and sweating, but far from finished. Hard living and harder training had kept them all in good shape.

"We're fine," Ethan said. "Nobody got hurt. Let's try and keep it that way."

The trailing edge of the second horde began to thin out, indicating that most of the ghouls who were capable of finding the gate had already done so. Ethan and Zeb held their men back, letting the walkers gain distance from the wall and congregate on open ground. Ethan had learned through hard experience that fighting in the open played to the strengths of the living—mainly speed and mobility—whereas close quarters combat gave an advantage to the dead. Just as he was opening his mouth to order an attack, Hicks held up a hand.

"Hey, hang on a minute boss," he said.

Ethan stopped, and looked at him expectantly. The stringy Texan's gaze drifted over to the ravine, a slight smile forming on his scarred face.

"Zeb, you mind if I borrow your horse for a minute? I got an idea."

The lawman glared skeptically, then shifted his attention to Ethan. "Sergeant?"

He shrugged. "Hey, your horse, your call."

Zeb frowned, but dismounted.

"All right, what's the plan?" Ethan asked.

"Y'all just head for the woods and hide. Zeb, keep an eye on me. When I signal, one o' y'all ride out and take this horse back to the trees with you."

Zeb looked at Hicks, then at Ethan, then back at Hicks. "Son, I sure hope you know what you're doing."

Hicks gave him a grin, handed his spear off to Ethan, and swung into the saddle. As he rode toward the horde, the others turned and made for cover behind the treeline.

Hicks spurred his borrowed mount in a wide circle around the ghouls, keeping the horse's speed at a low canter. In a few minutes, he managed to bunch the majority of ghouls into a cluster in the field between the wall and the ravine, then slowly began circling wider and wider, leading the horde toward the river. Ethan realized what was happening and grinned.

When the horde was within a few yards of the ravine's edge, Hicks slowed his horse to a walk, leaned forward, and whispered soothing words to calm the creature's ragged nerves. Raising a hand, he signaled to where Ethan and the others waited behind cover.

"I got it," Michael said, urging his mount forward. He broke cover and galloped toward the river.

Hicks dismounted, keeping an eye over his shoulder, and handed the reins over when Michael reached him. As the horses were led away, he maintained a brisk walk until the animals were out of sight. When he once again had the full attention of his audience, he began making his way down toward the water, waving and shouting as he went. Doggedly, with faces slack and arms outstretched for their prey, the infected began to follow him. Hicks quickly went out of sight, sliding down the hill with close to two dozen undead trailing after him. Ethan noticed that many of the walkers, unable to maintain their balance once they started down the hillside, toppled over as soon as they stepped over the edge.

Three times the crack of Hicks' rifle sounded, each time from a different location. From the reports, Ethan surmised that Hicks was moving closer to the bridge. When no more shots sounded for more than a minute, he began to worry. Images of Hicks being overwhelmed by ghouls and dying in agony gnawed at his mind, but he shook his head and dismissed them. If Hicks had been caught, they would have heard the screams. So he waited. And waited.

And waited.

Finally, just as Ethan was about to break cover and move in for a closer look, Hick's topped the rise at a sprint, clutching his

M-4 and sweating despite the cold. Ethan let out a breath. He motioned to his men. "Let's go. Switch to your rifles, and stay alert."

Hicks walked over to the others as they broke cover. "They're all in the ravine, boss," he said. "Ain't gettin' out any time soon."

"Good work. We'll have to remember that trick. Okay, everybody check your weapons, make sure you got rounds chambered and safeties off. Fingers off the trigger until you make contact. Hicks, you and Holland pair up. Cole, you're with me. Zeb, you know this place, right?"

The old man nodded. "Yep. Been here many a time."

"You mind taking point?"

"Not at all." He drew a big .357 revolver from hip and gestured to Hedges. "Chris, I believe it's your turn to watch the horses."

The deputy frowned but reached for the reins. "Be careful in there, Sheriff."

"Always am."

Michael sheathed his massive cleaver and drew a lever action rifle from behind his saddle. He checked the chamber, dismounted, and walked over to his uncle. "Ready when you are."

"All right. You boys stay behind me, and watch where you point them damn rifles. Any stray fire will be returned. Understood?"

Ethan smiled. "Don't worry. We've done this before."

Zeb grunted, and began walking toward the shattered entrance to Broken Bridge. Ethan had his men fan out in a diamond formation and followed. As they walked, his heart began to beat faster, and he felt a cold metallic taste form on the back of his tongue.

"Keep your eyes open," he said, more to himself than his men. "Maintain visual on each other at all times, and don't fucking go anywhere alone. We don't know what's waiting for us in there."

Cole chuckled. "Shit, man. When do we ever?"

Ethan looked up and saw the sun clearing the horizon to the east. A low bank of clouds hung over the hills in the distance, turning the sky the color of rust. Already the vultures were circling, indifferent to the men walking amongst the dead husks that would be their next meal.

As they grew closer to the wall, it seemed to rise up and loom over Ethan, heavy and forbidding. He remembered what it had felt like charging up the hill at Singletary Lake, bullets whipping past his ears, the undead groaning loud enough to rattle his teeth, men around him screaming as they fell, all the while wondering when it would be his turn, when a stray bullet would catch him and send him spinning to the ground.

Taking a deep breath, he focused his thoughts and cleared his mind as best he could. The old fear quieted, but stayed where it was, cold and gnawing. His father's voice drifted back to him from across the years, deep and strong. *Son, when you got a job to do, it's better to get it done than to stand around fearing it.*

Gritting his teeth, he squared his shoulders and walked on.

FIFTEEN

As Ethan suspected, the main gate wasn't really a gate at all.

Formed of several tons of concrete and steel, it was nothing more than a false front designed to fool attackers. It was, in fact, the strongest point of the town's defenses, heavily reinforced and bristling with machine guns. The purpose of its design was obvious: lure the enemy here, distract them by defending vigorously, and then flank the shit out of them. From the bullet holes, scorches, and scars along the outer defenses, Ethan guessed it had been an effective strategy.

Until now, at least.

After making a circuit of the inner perimeter, Ethan didn't spot any other entrances. He did, however, see plenty of rope ladders and primitive cranes, indicating these people had an escape plan, and at least some of them got away. His hopes of finding survivors began to grow.

What few infected they saw within the walls were mostly crawlers, along with a few crippled walkers too slow to make it out with the rest. Not wanting to waste time, Ethan and Cole killed them with headshots and left the corpses in the streets.

All around them, they saw the destruction left behind by the horde. Hundreds of dead bodies littered the ground—most of them obviously long dead—which made sense, considering the horde outside the gate had been mostly townsfolk. *But what happened to the rest of them, the horde that breached the town to begin with?*

It just didn't make sense. If this town was attacked recently, why weren't there more ghouls still wandering around? Usually, the infected stuck around for a few days after a kill, too distracted by the scent of fresh blood to move on. And in this case, it would be especially hard for the horde to escape because the shattered service entrance was the only way out. So what lured them away? Ethan gripped his rifle tighter, and kept moving.

Finished with their patrol, he and Cole returned to the entrance to find Zeb waiting for them. The old lawman was examining the shattered gate with a flashlight, shining it on broken hinges, twisted steel doors, and the singed archway. He spotted the two soldiers approaching and motioned them over.

"Sergeant, I need you to look at this."

Ethan stepped closer. "Sure. What do you got?"

"Look here." Zeb pointed at the bent and blasted remains of a three-inch steel plate. "You see those scorch marks, the shape of the distortion?"

"Yeah."

"This door was blown inward from the outside. Look at the arch. Those hinges weren't just broken, they were torn away. Whatever took this gate down, it ripped through three inches of steel and made it look easy. What kind of weapon could that, you reckon?"

Ethan blew out a sigh, not liking what he was hearing. "I'm not sure. RPGs wouldn't have been strong enough. Artillery, maybe, but the angle isn't right. Whatever hit this door, it did it straight on, like a bullet. Anybody pushing a cannon close enough to hit the gate at this angle would have been spotted."

He walked over to the other half of the door and squatted next to it, tracing a hand over a blackened, half-moon shaped hole in the middle. He thought back to Singletary Lake, and the large marauder compound the First Recon had raided there. Another squad had taken down the main gate, but he remembered what it looked like after they destroyed it. He was on the run at the time, and under heavy fire, but the memory stuck out clearly.

He also remembered the weapon that did it.

"If I had to guess," he said. "I'd say this was done with a LAW rocket."

Cole searched the scene, taking it in. After a moment, he ran a palm over his bald head and sighed. "You know, I think you might be right, man. If somebody got close enough, and had enough infected with them … but you'd have to be one crazy motherfucker to try it."

"Well," Zeb said, standing up. "This gate didn't blow itself up. Somebody did this intentionally, and with malice aforethought. If they used a rocket launcher to blow the gate, then that begs an obvious question."

Where did they get it, and do they have more? "There's another problem," Ethan said. "The infected we fought here are almost all townspeople. The corpses they killed in the fight are all older. Way older. How many people used to live here, Zeb?"

"The last census was about six months ago. They put it at two-hundred twenty, but I know for a fact some people joined up afterward."

Ethan nodded. "Sounds about right. I'd say we killed half of them in the field, and the other half are either crawlers, down in the ravine, or survivors who escaped."

Zeb's stoic mask began to crack, and his eyes filled with anger. "What kind of sick fuck would do something like this? They didn't even steal any weapons or supplies. All the caches are still locked up. Nothing's been taken. What the hell was the point?"

Ethan shook his head. "I don't know, Zeb. I've seen some crazy shit, but this…"

The three of them went silent. They stared at the gate for a while longer, as though standing in its presence might somehow unlock the mystery of its destruction. The silence became so oppressive that when Ethan's radio crackled in his ear, he almost screeched like a little girl.

"Alpha, Bravo, how copy?" It was Holland.

Cursing inwardly, and fighting down his racing heartbeat, he keyed the mike. "Copy loud and clear, Bravo. You find something? Over."

“Affirmative. We got a survivor, but I don’t think he’s going to last much longer. You might want to get over here fast.”

“Copy, Bravo. What’s your twenty?”

“North side of town, place looks like one of those pre-fab metal garages, only bigger. There’s a flagpole on the roof, but no flag. Should be easy to spot. Over.”

Ethan looked northward and saw the flagpole standing above the loose clusters of buildings less than a hundred yards away. “Copy. We’re on our way. Try to keep him breathing until we get there. Out.”

Zeb and Cole stared at him. The old sheriff’s eyes held a spark of hope. “Holland found a survivor. North side of town. We have to hurry.”

“Lead the way,” Zeb said. Ethan took off at a run.

Their passing caused a multitude of fleeting reflections to pass across the lifeless, staring eyes of the dead. High above them, the vultures continued circling, unabated and unconcerned. They were patient, those scavengers. There was no need for them to rush in, to risk landing when danger was nearby. They could stay right where they were, perfectly safe from harm until the loud, two-legged creatures below moved on.

Their meal wasn’t going anywhere.

*****

Holland waved to them from the roof.

The building he stood on was large and yellowish, and as he had said, it looked like a pre-fab steel garage, only about three times larger. The rolling doors were still intact, but a smaller side entrance lay bent and broken on the ground. Ethan entered first, shoving the battered door with his foot and sending it sliding across the concrete floor. As he walked inside, pale yellow sunlight filtered in through high windows, casting the room in a dull copper glow. The stench of rotting meat crawled into his throat, sticking in his nose and threatening to make him retch. Although he had smelled it hundreds of times, the odor of death still had the power to trigger his gag reflex.

"Over this way, boss."

Ethan looked to his right and saw Hicks clinging to a ladder descending from a trapdoor in the ceiling. Ethan raised a hand. Hicks nodded once and climbed back up.

Looking around, he couldn't tell what the building's original purpose had been, but the people of Broken Bridge had converted it into a barracks. Rows of wooden bunk beds and footlockers lay all around in broken, overturned disarray. The kitchen area near the back was in shambles, and several nearby tables lay flat on the ground as though crushed by a massive hand. Thick, rust-colored streaks smeared the concrete from one end to the other, splattered on overturned beds and scattered sheets. Patches of ripped-out hair, torn gobbets of flesh, and discarded bones littered the ground.

Ethan spotted something in the shadows a few feet away and clicked on the small tactical light attached to his rifle. When he raised the beam, he saw a single amputated thumb standing on end, propped up on its ragged stump. It pointed straight up in the air, as though offering a cheerful welcome to the reeking slaughterhouse and the horrors within. Ethan grimaced and kicked it away.

He turned his head and spoke over his shoulder. "Come on. Let's get to the roof."

The others followed behind him, eyes wide and hands tight on their weapons. Every few feet, they spotted the remains of crawlers Hicks or Holland had put down during their sweep. One of them was missing its arms and legs, and the rest were so mangled they were almost unrecognizable as human.

"The infected must have got in here," Cole said, stating the obvious.

"But where are all the bodies?" Michael replied.

Zeb spoke up. "Either outside the gate where we killed 'em, or trapped in the riverbed. 'Cept for those poor bastards." He gestured at a dead crawler.

Ethan led the way up the ladder, emerging from the gloomy interior into the rapidly brightening morning. A few feet away, Holland knelt beside a man who lay propped against Hick's backpack. The man's clothes were torn and bloody, and one of his hands lay in his lap, swaddled in a thick wrapping of bloodied bandages. Holland poured water from his canteen into a metal cup and held it to the man's lips. The man reached up with a trembling hand and drank from it, but pushed it away after a few swallows, sputtering and coughing.

"Alan!" Zeb said, emerging from the trapdoor and rushing over.

The man lying on the ground looked up groggily. "Sheriff Austin? That you?"

"It's me, Alan," he said, kneeling. "What happened to you?"

Alan reached up with his good hand and gripped Zeb's sleeve. "I got bit. Don't have much time left-" Another coughing fit wracked him, and Zeb had to wait a few moments while the stricken man caught his breath. "Listen," he finally managed to croak. "You need to know what happened here."

Zeb's face went tight. He gripped Alan's hand in both of his and held on. "I'm listening."

"There was a horde. Had to be over a thousand strong. They got through the gate last night around midnight."

"How?" Ethan asked. He was fairly certain about his rocket launcher theory, but wanted to know for sure. "What destroyed the gate? Did you see it?"

Alan shook his head wearily. "No. I was on watch at the southern wall, wasn't close enough to see what happened. I caught a flash of light and heard a sound like a gunshot, only a hell of a lot louder. Then there was an explosion. Powerful as hell, my ears are still ringing from it. Blew the gate right off its hinges. The next thing I know, everybody's sounding the alarm and there's infected pouring in like a flood."

"What about the charges on the bridge?" Zeb asked. "Why weren't they triggered?"

Alan's eyes opened wider. "Some bastard killed the guards at the gate. Scrawny fucker in a big coat, dressed like one of us. He knifed 'em both, then the infected got 'em. I saw it happen, but I was too far away to stop it. I tried to shoot the fucker, but he ran off too quick."

Ethan felt a creeping coldness start in his gut, spread through his arms, and tingle its way up to his face. He thought about the front gate, and the blast marks, and the absence of the horde that destroyed the town. Looking at it from a distance, the pieces began to fit.

"They were the only ones close enough to throw the switch," Alan went on. "By the time I got there, the dead were everywhere. We tried to hold them at the gate, but there were too many of 'em. They broke our line, and everybody fell back. It was pitch dark, most of the torches were out. We were fighting blind all the way back to the southern wall. I got cut off and had to duck into the barracks. Bunch of other people followed me in, but we couldn't all get up the ladder fast enough. They tried to hold their ground, but the dead just kept packing in tighter and tighter. I was the first one up, but by the time I reached the roof, everybody else was dead or dying."

Alan stopped to take a few wheezing breaths and a sip of water. His face was ghostly pale, his lips so blue they were almost translucent, sweat standing out in beads on his forehead. The shivers gripping him were rapidly devolving into convulsions, and his eyes were beginning to glaze over. Grimacing against the pain, he continued.

"The man at the gate, the one who killed the guards, he's the one who did this. He led those ghouls here. He destroyed the gate somehow, and he turned them loose in the compound. You have to find him before he does it again, Zeb. You heard about them other towns, right? It can't be a coincidence."

"Are there any other survivors?" Holland asked impatiently. "Did you see anyone else escape?"

Alan turned his head, blinking lazily. "I don't know. It was too dark, I could barely see my hand in front of my face. I tried calling out for a while after that son-of-a-bitch led the horde away, but nobody answered. Maybe the children got away over the north wall. I don't know."

The dying man turned his gaze back to Zeb and leaned forward, eyes bright. "He was *laughing*, Zeb. I heard him. While those monsters killed us all, he was sitting on top of the market shelter, swinging his feet like a little kid and fucking *laughing*. You find that bastard, Zeb. You find him, and you make him pay for what he did. You hear me? Promise me you'll find that motherfucker."

Zeb patted the man's shoulder gently, but there was no softness in his eyes. "I promise, Alan. I'll find him, and when I do, I'll make him suffer. You have my word on that."

Alan seemed reassured. He lay back down, his grip weakening in Zeb's hand. In a few short minutes, he lost consciousness, and then rattled out his last breath. Zeb reached gently down and shut the dead man's eyes.

"Uncle Zeb," Michael said. "You know what we need to do."

The old sheriff nodded slowly and stood up. He took a few steps away and rubbed the back of his hand over his forehead. "You mind doin' it, son? I don't know if I got the heart."

Michael gripped his uncle's shoulder. "I'll take care of it."

Ethan motioned to his men to step away and pulled Hick's pack from under Alan's trembling body. Already, he was showing signs of reanimation.

"Go ahead."

Michael drew a small pistol from under his coat and stepped forward. "I'm sorry Alan. I wish we could have gotten here sooner." He raised his hand and pulled the trigger.

Birds took flight under a golden haze as the gunshot echoed into the morning.

*****

They spent the rest of the day looking for other survivors, but found only corpses.

At the edge of the wall where Ethan and Cole found the ladders and cranes, they discovered a semicircle of dead bodies stacked waist-high. Upon examining them, Ethan realized they were all the older, more ruined bodies of the horde that destroyed the town.

Behind them was a set of bunkhouses similar to the large barracks where they had found Alan, but smaller. Zeb explained that all of the town's children slept in the bunkhouses near the escape apparatus, just in case. From what Ethan could see, it looked as if a group of defenders had formed a line around the children and held it while they escaped, but later succumbed to the horde. The ground in front of the wall was covered in a carpet of empty shell casings and broken hand weapons.

Ethan nudged a few of them with his boot and thought of his own son back at Fort Bragg. Andrea was probably cooking breakfast right then, sunlight shining in through the kitchen window and setting her bright red hair aglow. Aiden would have woken up hours ago, coloring in his books, playing with his toys, and asking when daddy was coming home. Ethan looked up at the sun, the same warmth shining on him and his distant family, and he tried very hard not to cry.

After exploring the ground outside the south wall, Zeb and Hedges found more than a dozen unique tracks leading across the overgrown field to the forest beyond. Most of them were small, but there were a few adult sized ones as well.

"Well, at least the children got away," Ethan said when Hedges delivered the news.

"We'll light a signal fire for them tonight," the deputy replied. "If they're still nearby, they'll come back. You might want to have your men lay low, Sergeant. Those kids have a couple of defenders with them, and after what happened here last night, they might react badly to unfamiliar faces. You should probably let me and Zeb do the talking."

Ethan nodded. "Fine by me. We'll stay out of your way."

Tired from a long day of fruitless searching, Ethan decided to pack it in for the night. After rounding up his men, he ordered them to restock their ammo from the town's armory—Zeb had found the key to it on Alan's body and opened it up to them—then scavenge some food and find a spot to make camp. Cole suggested the roof of an old fast-food restaurant near the eastern wall, well away from Zeb's signal fire near the gate. They all agreed.

"What about water?" Hicks asked. "Ain't like we can take it from the river."

Ethan thought about the ghouls splashing around in the muddy stream and grimaced. "You're right. We need to refill our canteens. Cole, let's go take a look around and see what we can find. Hicks, you and Holland find some food and get a meal going."

"Will do, boss."

In a house less than a block down the street, Cole found a black plastic barrel with the words DRINKING WATER in white stencil across the front. Opening the lid, he leaned down and sniffed.

"Yep. That's water." He turned to look at Ethan. "Think it's safe?"

"I don't see why it wouldn't be. We'll filter it and boil it anyway, just to be sure."

They loaded the barrel onto a hand truck they found nearby and wheeled it back to camp. Hicks had found a small metal fire pit and hauled it to the roof, along with a few bundles of wood. Holland got a fire going, and set to work making a stew from jars of preserved vegetables and dried venison liberated from the town's emergency supply. Ethan smelled the food and felt his stomach grumble, realizing he hadn't eaten since before dawn. It was now nearly sunset.

They ate their meal in subdued silence, each man staring straight down at his food and thinking his own dark thoughts. Ethan finished his first bowl quickly and went back for another, eating it more slowly this time. He kept his mind on setting up the watch rotation, making sure everyone cleaned their weapons after dinner, and wondering how many survivors were going to come back through the gate that night. He did his best not to look around at the town, at what less than two days ago had been a thriving community, a place where hundreds of Outbreak survivors had carved out a life for themselves wishing only for peace and a safe place to raise their children. All gone now.

He thought about the destroyed gate, and the shape of the blasted doors, and the scorches on the archway. He thought about Alan, and his last words admonishing Zeb to find the person responsible for the death of this place. He thought about Alan's description of the killer, a scrawny knife-wielding man in a big coat. He thought about the trail they had followed to Broken Bridge, and the fact that very few of the attacking horde had remained behind. If the horde was still following the madman responsible for all this mayhem, it wouldn't be hard to pick up their trail again. Once they did, they might be able to figure out where the murderer leading the horde planned to strike next.

Tomorrow, he would talk to Zeb. If the old lawman was half as smart as Ethan thought he was, he had most likely come to the same conclusions.

It was a place to start.

SIXTEEN

Gideon felt like whistling.

He couldn't, of course. Whistling was an activity he'd left in the past, along with half of his teeth. A few key dental structures removed and one of a man's most basic expressions, making music, was gone.

Still, he smiled as he walked. Even the gaps between his last few crumbling teeth couldn't dampen his spirits. He felt light as a feather, twisting and dancing on the air. Whistling might not have been an option, but there were plenty of other things a man could do to entertain himself.

Killing was one of them.

Smoking meth was another. For Gideon, the two were inextricably blended.

The town of Broken Bridge was miles behind him, a mission accomplished beyond his wildest expectations. It was a larger place than any other he'd attempted to strike, and when his finger fell on the trigger of the rocket launcher, Gideon was sure his time was finally up. No part of him expected to see the heavy gate fall so spectacularly, and his gap-toothed smile widened as he remembered the thick metal ripping away from the concrete supporting it.

Broken Bridge had been a place of order and discipline. At least that was what the people he captured had told him. A group of stranded soldiers had built the town, gathered other survivors together, armed them, trained them, and turned them into a small but lethal militaristic society. They had a fierce reputation, those people, and even the most daring marauders no longer bothered them.

A daunting task, killing such worthy opponents.

When Gideon struck, a swarm of ghouls at his back, it was with the expectation that he would die. High as he had been, and drunk on the rush of his own impending death, the sense of unreality gripping him had heightened to levels he'd never known. The amphetamines drove him, gave him the energy he needed to push past the pain, and the exhaustion, and his own flagging strength. He'd felt so goddamn *powerful.* But below that surreal elation, always burning bright and hot within him, was the anger.

The memories hit him again as he walked in the pre-dawn light. The fledgling brightness of the morning sun dimmed, going dark as he heard the echo of his long-dead doctor's voice. The day when everything changed.

HIV, his doctor had said. *Bad news, to be sure, and expensive to treat. But it's not the death sentence it used to be.*

He'd almost hit the man then. Not a death sentence, sure. But a lifetime of medicine and ridiculous precautions because of *one* night away from home. Because he'd been lonely and horny and had taken a risk. In what universe was that fair?

Rather than get violent, Gideon had clenched his teeth and listened. He heard the spiel about opportunistic infections, proper drug regiments, taking precautions. He kept calm by imagining how surprised the doctor's face would look if he slammed a fist into his jaw. Or how unruffled the good doctor would be if Gideon jammed a dirty needle into his arm, all the while chanting about how it wasn't a death sentence.

The world darkened a little more, in reality this time, as clouds moved in. Gideon thought it appropriate. The memories stung now more than ever—the other half of the equation that kept him running.

Julia left him as soon as he broke the news. She'd suspected his infidelity for years; no wife whose husband stayed gone on business trips as long as he did could do otherwise. She screamed at him, called him names, threw things, all over one mistake. Gideon held himself in check.

Julia cursed him as she dragged her suitcase to the front door. He tried to stop her, reason with her. He felt the razor-sharp memory of his hand squeezing her arm as she pushed him, trying to make him let go. He squeezed harder, pulling her away from the door.

Until then, he had managed to bottle up the rage, the injustice of it. All his life had been a lesson in channeling those impulses into more productive behavior. But when she slapped him, teeth bared with the effort of swinging her arm as hard as she could, his vision went red. There was a short gap, a flashpoint where time passed but no memories penetrated the haze.

The next thing he remembered, Julia was standing over him, her back against the door as she clutched her bleeding face. Gideon's left eye hurt like ten kinds of hell, and his balls ached all the way to his teeth.

Julia left that day, and it was the last time he ever saw her. There was no pity on her face, nothing of the love and adoration he'd seen on their wedding day. Staring up at her then, he would have accepted fear or anger or even hate.

Instead, she had sneered at him and called him a fucking coward.

From there, the memories grew vague. He kept up with the medications because, no matter how dark the horizon, Gideon could be relied upon to protect Gideon. A lesser man might have fallen to pieces and crawled to others, begging for help or sympathy.

Gideon took another path.

He got trashed.

Months of working extra hours and hoarding cash were punctuated by breaks filled to the brim with hedonism to make the Romans blush. When he planned those forays, there was never any intent to do anything stupid. But once the booze soaked his brain, considerations like telling women his HIV status or even wearing protection became unimportant.

When the world fell apart, he was coming off one of his benders. He'd missed the news, having spent over a week in an expensive hotel room drinking, snorting cocaine, and banging whores. It didn't help that he had shattered the TV on the first night.

It wasn't quite instantaneous, but when Gideon dried out enough to leave the room and heard the newscasts, he began to worry. The talking heads said it all, how the dead were rising, how the infection was spreading, how the chaos was building like a storm. The President assured everyone the military would soon have the situation under control. *Stay in your homes,* he said. *Don't panic.*

Gideon was a lot of things, but stupid wasn't one of them. He could read between the lines; the plague was out of control. Things were getting bad, and quickly.

When the Outbreak hit Gideon's town, he was long gone, running ahead of the storm with a trunk full of medicine stolen from every pharmacy he could rob. Two days and a gun to his head later, the car and his pills were gone.

On foot, the plague caught up to him. Gideon found himself in the middle of it, surviving despite the odds. He'd done so for a long time, now.

After the first few weeks of trying, he gave up searching for the right medications. He wasn't truly sick, then, but he knew it was only a matter of time. So he'd gone wandering, surviving day to day, eventually finding a measure of peace.

Until he found the meth.

The house had looked normal enough on the ground floor, but when he'd gone down to the basement, the normalcy ended. Whoever had set up the lab knew what they were doing. It wasn't one of those filthy, cluttered death traps he'd seen on the news so many times. This setup was clean, orderly, professional. Clearly labeled chemicals, properly stored. A set of beakers and burners that would have been right at home in a high-school science lab. And sitting on a shelf, separated into bundles packaged tightly together with clear cellophane, was the meth.

Hundreds of pounds of it.

Gideon couldn't even guess at the street value. He'd always been partial to cocaine, but hey, any port in a storm. He'd taken all he could carry. After smoking some and feeling the tingling rush of strength that came with an amphetamine high, he realized he could carry more. So he went back and stocked up again until his pack had bulged with the stuff.

It wasn't nearly as heavy as it used to be.

Slowing his pace, he wandered over to a large stone on the side of the road and sat down, warming himself in the sun. The thin glass pipe no longer burned his fingers when he smoked, calluses having long since formed in curious lines across his fingertips.

The swarm followed, and the fresh sense of hyper-reality brought on by the atomized crystal flowing into his lungs made the ghouls stand out even more sharply against the lovely day. His memories since beginning his habit were vague in many places, but when he lit the pipe, those first days came back in vivid detail.

What began as an escape—a break from the fear that every little cough and sniffle would be the illness that ate him alive—had evolved into a crushing addiction. Just as Gideon had no way to know when HIV would transition into AIDS, he didn't feel the damage from the drugs building up inside of him.

The psychosis took root in his already anger-ridden mind, brain chemistry and structure irrevocably altered by time and the painful memories of his life before the Outbreak. Whatever tenuous grip he'd had on sanity loosened bit by bit until, finally, it fell away altogether.

That was when the killing started.

At first, it was runners. People out on their own with no permanent place to live. A few here and there, mostly after arguments. Those early kills were crimes of passion and opportunity, fueled by hate and justified by his situation. As time went on, his psychosis grew worse and worse, and as a consequence, so did his crimes.

Gideon watched the swarm and planned his next move. Broken Bridge had been the end game. The finale. His tomb as well as his greatest accomplishment. After all, he had survived the end of the world only to face a future limited by the disease slowly dissolving his immune system.

He sat on the rock and watched the swarm grow larger. The high wasn't as powerful as he'd have liked—the plight of the junkie—but it was enough. It quieted the hungry thing entwined in his brain. Had a person approached him then and asked *why* he did the things he did, the question would have brought only a blank stare. Purely hypothetical, of course, as he hadn't allowed a person close enough to speak without killing them for months.

If he had to die, why should anyone else be allowed to live?

The monster inside him purred at the thought, wanted to know how to proceed. Gideon shouldered his rifle—a military sniper carbine stolen from the body of a dead soldier—and stood, full of energy. He didn't know where to go from here, hadn't planned for victory.

But he knew what he'd like to do. Better, he knew where to ask the right questions.

*****

"I want to know where the people are," Gideon said in an even, almost bored voice. "I asked your friends, but they didn't answer."

The clearing was strewn with bodies, but the swarm would be on its way soon to clean up the mess. Gideon never let them get too far behind. They were so easily distracted, his little darlings. The loud crack of the rifle—three fast shots to take out the guard, and one a few seconds later to lame the woman—would draw their attention.

The rest was knife work.

Five people killed, and easily done at that. One dead man to start, one injured woman clutching at the spurt of blood jetting from her leg, and the same question asked for each of them before they died. The next two were teenagers, too rebellious to do more than spit in his face. His weapon cowed them, but not enough to make them give in.

Two quick slashes, and the mud turned red around them.

The other pair of corpses were an older couple, too horrified to even attempt to answer when Gideon spoke to them. Which led him to the woman, who now had a belt cinched tight around her thigh and her hands tied behind her back. Gideon straddled her stomach.

“Hey,” he said, tapping the woman on the forehead with a crusty fingernail. “I'm waiting. Talk to me. Where are the people?”

She stared at him, terrified, but with a defiant gleam in her sky-blue eyes. “Fuck you. You're going to kill me anyway. Just do it.”

“That's true,” Gideon replied. “You're gonna die, that’s for sure. But it's up to you how much pain you feel before then.”

The woman glanced at his crotch, eyes widening. Gideon laughed.

“Sorry, sweetheart, but that's not gonna happen. That old thing stopped being much use a long time ago.” He fumbled around the pockets of his coat, stained with the juices of the dead man he'd pulled it from, and eventually produced a small butane torch. He clicked it to life.

“I want to know where the people are,” Gideon repeated as he held the blade of his small knife to the blue-white flame.

The woman's breathing quickened, but she closed her mouth into a tight line. Gideon cocked his head at the display of self-control, birdlike in his curiosity. Without changing expression, he pressed the flat of the blade against her cheek, the tip just below her eye.

Skin sizzled, the smell somewhere between chicken and bacon. He pulled the blade away when the sound stopped, not bothering to ask again. The monster wanted pain and Gideon agreed with it, and both of them were dangerously close to forgetting their purpose.

A second, louder wave of sizzling was broken by the woman's pent-up scream. Gideon stared at her as she shrieked in agony, wonder and confusion on his face.

For a fraction of a second, the person he used to be took over. Just for a flash of time, he saw her for what she was: a victim. Pity came along for the ride, an emotion so dusty and unfamiliar he couldn't reconcile it with the furious hatred driving him. Then the random firing of long unused synapses ended, and Gideon leaned in once more.

"I'd like to say I won't ask you again," he said, grinning. "But the truth is, we've got some time before my friends show up, and I'm having fun. So please, feel free to stay quiet."

"No!" the woman shrieked, her breath fanning out his lank hair. "North. Go north about five miles. You'll come to a little fort off the highway. A town a few miles northeast of here uses it as a trade depot. Watch long enough, you'll be able to follow them back home."

A tear rolled down her cheek at the admission. Gideon darted in and flicked his tongue across the droplet.

"Thank you," he said with genuine warmth. "You runners and your little camp sites. All of you share them, keep them in good shape. It's like shooting fish in a barrel. Even animals are smart enough to look for prey at the watering hole."

Gideon put the tip of the knife against her chest at an angle. Slowly, so slowly, he pushed until the blade slid between the ribs, its back scraping against the sternum. The woman screamed, tried to get away, but he had practice at this.

He stopped the blade when he felt resistance.

"The point is sitting against your heart," he said casually. "An ounce of pressure and you'll be gone in a minute. During that time, you should think about how stupid animals are. Always going back to their safe little places no matter how often the wolves attack them there."

With her last ounce of strength, the woman followed the example set by the murdered teenagers and spit in Gideon's face.

"They all do that," he said, and pushed.

*****

Hours after the swarm cleaned the flesh from the bones of his victims, Gideon found himself cleaning the blood from his knife again. The small town was right where it was supposed to be. There was even a group packing up from a trade when he got there. An older man and two young women. Gideon repeated his trick, now getting stale and not as much fun.

The older of the two girls gave him detailed information about the nearby community. More a city, from what she'd told him. Hundreds of people, a huge wall, but no interior defenses. A fortress on the outside but soft in the middle. A perfect target.

"Steel City," Gideon muttered, pushing greasy locks off his face. His hand came back red. The last few minutes with the girl had gotten ... intense.

He said the name again, rolling it around on his tongue. Only now that his blood began to calm, and what passed for rationality began to reassert itself, did he wonder why the place was called that. He glanced down at the rapidly cooling corpse on the ground and felt a small pang of regret. Not at the murder—that was as close as he came to pleasure nowadays—but that he hadn't asked her to explain.

It nagged at him, but the monster inside took over. That was how he saw it, at least. In a dark corner of his mind rarely exposed to light and certainly never visited, Gideon knew the truth. Whatever destruction had befallen his brain, it had only distorted and magnified what was already there.

The monster was him, a version of him freed from the shackles of his already shaky conscience by severe neurological trauma. Had Gideon the bravery to admit it, he might have managed enough control to end his life without more mayhem.

But a lifetime of being a bully, of lying to himself, of fantasizing about all the ways he could avenge perceived slights, had created conditions perfect for a monster to grow. Gideon could be relied on to protect Gideon, after all.

Even from himself.

SEVENTEEN

At 0700 hours, Cole grabbed Ethan by the toes of his right foot and shook vigorously. Ethan came up swinging, as he always did, but this time he didn't hit anyone. Cole had already backed off a few steps, remembering very well the last time he'd stood too close to his friend after waking him up. Ethan came back to himself, eyes clearing, and cursed.

"I gotta stop doing that. I'm gonna hurt somebody one of these days."

"S'cool, man." Cole smiled. "No hard feelings. Happens all the time."

"Not to you."

Cole shrugged, his smile fading. "Looks like the survivors came back."

Ethan climbed out of his bedroll, got to his feet, and looked where Cole was pointing. Zeb and his men were approaching, followed by a group of armed, hard-faced children and two adults, also armed and grim-looking. Most of the children were tweens and teenagers, but there were a few toddlers as well, the smallest of them being carried by older children.

"Jesus Christ."

"Hey man, at least they're still alive."

"What's going on?"

Ethan looked over his shoulder and saw Holland struggling out of his tent.

"Zeb's on his way. The survivors are with him."

"The kids?"

"Yep."

Holland groaned and sank back down into his sleeping bag. "Wake me up when it's time to move out."

Ethan ran a hand over his face while Cole chuckled beside him. "Isaac, get these guys up and moving, please. I'm going to go have a word with the good sheriff."

"Cool."

After slipping on his boots, Ethan rinsed his mouth out with water from his canteen, spit it over the edge of the roof, and climbed down the ladder. He knew he must look a sight with his red-rimmed eyes and short, scruffy beard. But right then, he just didn't give a shit.

When he reached the bottom of the ladder, Zeb spoke up first, waving a hand at the two adults accompanying the children. "Sergeant Thompson, this is Alicia Meyer and Omar Terrell. They were guarding the children last night when the swarm hit."

Ethan raised a hand in acknowledgment, nodding once. Now that they were closer, he could see the survivors' exhaustion as clear as day. They wavered on their feet, unsteady with dehydration and hunger, none of them looking as though they had slept a wink in the last twenty-four hours. The adults had the haunted, gaunt-faced look of having suffered severe mental trauma: the thousand-yard stare. Ethan had seen it many times, both on other people and looking back at him in the mirror, but the sight of it never stopped twisting in his chest.

When he shifted his gaze to the children, he saw a mixture of anger and fear tightly hidden under an ingrained watchfulness. Their eyes darted left, right, up, down, the same conical pattern used by soldiers to scan large environments for signs of hostiles. Each of them clutched a weapon, ranging from small-caliber firearms to bows-and-arrows, and even a few handmade crossbows. Some of the older children had simple melee weapons such as woodcutting axes, machetes, or crowbars strung across their backs. All in all, they looked like a formidable little fighting force. And again, looking at their dirty, angel faces, Ethan had to try very hard not to cry.

"Do any of you need medical attention?" he asked, clearing his throat.

The woman, Alicia, glanced at him skeptically. "You a doctor?"

"No. I'm a medic. Used to be an EMT back before the Outbreak."

Her skepticism faded, and she went back to just looking tired. "Thanks for the offer, but we're fine. Nothing a little food, water, and rest won't fix. I'm more concerned about the immediate future." She inclined her head slightly toward the children behind her.

It occurred to Ethan that on their walk from the main gate, the children must have undoubtedly seen the carpet of dead bodies littering the streets. Most of the corpses belonged to the horde that destroyed Broken Bridge, but at least a few of them were neighbors or relatives. Parents even. Although it was tragic, he was glad his team had put down most of the reanimated townsfolk outside the gate where the children couldn't see them. *Small mercies.*

"I understand there are emergency supply caches here, correct?" Ethan asked.

"Yes, but that's not what I'm worried about. This town isn't safe anymore, not without the gate intact or…"

Or the other two-hundred people who used to live here. "Is there a fallback point or an emergency shelter you can use for the time being?"

"The roof of the main barracks is the safest spot in town. We could shelter there for a few days, but we won't be able to stay for long. As soon as word gets out about what happened here, every raider for miles is going to come running. There's still a lot of weapons, ammo, and food stashed around here. It'll be a free-for-all. We don't want to be here when that happens."

Ethan nodded. "Maybe I can help with that. Give me a few minutes, I'll be right back."

Back on the roof, he powered up his radio and hailed FOB Harkin. The same bored private answered, but didn't give him any grief this time before fetching Colonel Lanning.

“Sergeant Thompson, what can I do for you?”

“Broken Bridge has been overrun sir.”

There was a long silence. “What happened?”

Ethan related the events of the previous day: finding Alan dying on a rooftop, exploring the ruined town, and the plight of the few survivors. He also explained about the madman leading the horde around, and his theory that Broken Bridge’s fate had been the same to befall the other towns that had gone dark. When he finished, he had to wait a long time for Lanning to respond.

“That’s a hell of a mess you got there, Sergeant,” he said, finally.

“Yes sir, it is. My immediate concern is for the survivors. Most of them are children. I know our resources are stretched thin, but we can’t just leave them here.”

“Wouldn’t dream of it. As it happens, we have some extra air assets on hand, as well as two companies from the 82nd Airborne. They’re here en route to Fort Bragg, just got done handling some unpleasant business up in Kentucky. I can have two Chinooks on their way to you within the hour. How many men do you need?”

Ethan thought about it for a moment. In addition to escorting these people to safety, he wanted to move their supplies and equipment along with them. The two Chinooks could handle that, but it would take a long time and require a lot of hard work. He said as much to Colonel Lanning.

“Is Broken Bridge still viable?” Lanning asked.

“What do you mean, sir?”

“Are the defenses still intact? Can people still live there?”

“For the most part, yes. The problem is the main gate; it’s completely destroyed. That, and all the dead bodies.”

“Not a problem. I can have a Facilitator and a construction crew there within forty-eight hours. Best case, they’ll have that gate good as new in no time, and at worst, they’ll just wall it up until we can send a team of engineers. Central has been looking for a place to put an FOB out that way for months now. If those folks are agreeable, we might have just found our site."

Ethan was surprised; he hadn't expected to get that much help. But he couldn't deny it was a good idea. "I'll ask them, sir. Something tells me they won't turn you down."

"I'll be here."

After a quick conversation with Alicia, he got the authorization he needed. The relief on Alicia's face made Ethan's chest hurt. He relayed the information to Lanning.

"Excellent," the Colonel said. "I'll get the Chinooks in the air ASAP with as many men as they can carry. They'll be under orders to get to work straightaway cleaning out the dead and repairing the main gate. I'll radio Central and let them know what's going on. You need me to contact Lieutenant Jonas and fill him in for you, Sergeant?"

"That would be helpful sir. One thing though, I can't hang around to wait for reinforcements."

"Why not?"

"The horde that destroyed this place is on the move, sir. The man leading it is still out there, and I have reason to believe he may try to do something like this again."

Another silence. "That's a good point. What do you want to do about it?"

Ethan relaxed a little. He'd half expected Lanning to order him to return to his unit, and dispatch an attack helicopter to find the horde and disperse it. Which honestly wasn't a bad idea, but the more pressing matter was finding the man responsible for destroying Broken Bridge. The twice-dead corpses outside the gate had once been good people, and they deserved justice. Their children deserved justice. Ethan planned to make sure they got it.

"That horde isn't getting any closer," he said. "We need to go after it and find out where it's headed. If we find the horde, we can find the person responsible for what happened here."

"You need air support?"

"Not yet. If our man spots a helicopter, he might get spooked and go to ground. If that happens, we'll never find him. For now, it's best if he doesn't know we're on to him."

"Makes sense to me. What about the survivors? Is someone in charge there?"

"Yes sir, a woman. Her name is Alicia Meyer. Average height, medium build, Caucasian, late thirties to early forties, dark hair. She and one other adult are looking after the children."

"Very well, I'll pass along the description. I assume you'll be moving out after the horde."

"Yes sir. Just as soon as I'm off the line with you."

"All right then, Sergeant. Watch your ass out there. Get your men back in one piece."

"I'll do my best, sir. Talk to you soon."

*****

Alicia waited with Zeb while Ethan and his men removed the corpses from the main barracks, swept aside the severed body parts, and washed Alan's blood and brains off the roof. They knew the children had probably seen their share of gruesome things, but still, the soldiers wanted to spare them as much horror as they could, even if only to make themselves feel better about leaving them behind.

Once the survivors had settled in on the roof, Ethan gave Alicia a smoke flare. "The helicopters will be coming in from the northeast," he said. "When they get close, pop this flare and throw it on the rooftop next door. They'll most likely set down outside the main gate, but you want them to see your location from the sky. When they approach, have everyone keep their weapons out of sight. These guys just got back from a combat mission, so they're probably jumpy. Some of them might react badly if you guys show up armed."

Alicia nodded and looked down, turning the flare over in her hands. She had black circles under her eyes and congealed blood in her hair. It was all Ethan could do not to wrinkle his nose at the smell, but still he had to fight the urge to put his arms around her.

"Thank you, Sergeant," she said. "For everything."

The sunrise cut through her blue eyes as she looked up, translucent irises glittering like flecks of ice. Ethan forced a smile. "It's the least I could do. Good luck, ma'am." With that, he turned and climbed down the ladder. His men followed.

Zeb and his men rode a circle around town trying to pick up the horde's trail. It didn't take them very long; the swarm had flattened a massive swath of undergrowth along an old gravel farm road. Hedges rode back and found Ethan near the main gate.

"Looks like they're headed north," he said, swinging down from the saddle.

"Any towns out that way?" Ethan replied.

"There's a couple of small camps used by runners and a trading post off the highway, but the nearest town is Steel City."

"How far?"

"About twenty miles. You think that's where our man is headed?

Ethan rubbed a hand along the back of his neck and let out a sigh. "Could be. We'll worry about that later. For now, we need to follow this trail and try to get ahead of him."

Hedges nodded. "All right. I'll go round up the others and grab some supplies, then we'll get going."

"Sounds like a plan."

They followed the trail for a few miles until they came upon a set of railroad tracks running parallel to the road. Zeb asked everyone to stay put for a few minutes, then rode out to scout the way ahead. When he returned, he was urging his mount at a canter and practically jumping in his saddle.

"I know these tracks," he said. "Used 'em last year to escort a caravan from Broken Bridge to Steel City. Can't believe I forgot about it. If the horde is headed for Steel City, we can use these tracks to get ahead of it."

"You sure?" Ethan asked.

"Yep. It's a straight shot, all the bridges are intact, and it'll spit us out less than a mile south of town. We can pick up the highway there, and be at the gates before sundown if we hurry."

Ethan turned to his men. "Cole, mark this location on GPS, upload it to the tablet, and radio FOB Harkin. Hicks, find us a spot to cache our gear. We're traveling light from here on out—water, weapons, and ammo only. Leave everything else behind except the comms gear. We can come back for it later."

Zeb nodded his approval and swung down from the saddle. "Mike, Chris, we need to muffle the horses hooves. They're going to be loud as hell on those rail ties. If that horde comes near, I don't want them to hear us." He reached into a saddlebag, pulled out a blanket, and began cutting it into squares. Hedges and Michael did the same until they had four squares each, then they wrapped the material around the horses' hooves and tied them off at the ankles.

Ethan and his men returned from caching their packs to find the others mounted up and ready to go. They set a brisk pace, the horses plodding ahead at a slow trot and the four soldiers moving double-time. After five miles, Cole—being the biggest of them by far—began to show signs of fatigue. His massive strength, an advantage in almost every other situation, turned out to be a liability now that speed was their primary concern. All that muscle was useful, but required lots of oxygen. He began to lag farther and farther behind until Ethan finally asked Zeb to slow down.

"Y'all go on ahead," Cole huffed, sweating profusely. "I'll catch up."

"No can do," Ethan replied. "We go together, or we don't go at all. Can you keep up a brisk walk?" Cole ground his teeth and nodded.

They carried on at a slower pace for a few hours. The sun arced through the sky overhead, tracing its path toward evening. They stopped only once to water the horses and wolf down a quick meal. Zeb was obviously frustrated they weren't making better time, but as it turned out, slowing down worked to their advantage. Just after crossing a short trestle over a creek, Hicks tapped Ethan on the shoulder. "Hey boss."

"Yeah?"

"Look over there."

He craned his head, saw what Hicks was pointing at, and nearly tripped over his own feet.

"Holy shit."

Hicks grunted.

"Zeb," he hissed, pitching his voice low. The lawman kept riding.

"*Zeb.*" Sharper this time.

He stopped and turned around in the saddle, his expression irritated. "What?"

Ethan stabbed a finger to his left three times, and then placed it over his lips. Zeb bent down to peer below a few branches obstructing his view, saw what Ethan was gesturing at, and went still. The color drained from his face.

"Dear God," he whispered.

Parallel to the tracks, maybe two-hundred yards down the gently sloping valley, was the horde.

Ethan guessed there had to be over a thousand of them, weaving, stumbling, and lurching through the forest. Distantly, he heard a faint clacking sound.

"You hear that?" he whispered.

Hicks nodded. "Yep. Sounds like somebody hittin' sticks together."

Realizing what that meant, Ethan raised an arm and waved to Holland. For once, the diminutive soldier didn't roll his eyes as he came over.

"You hear that noise?" Ethan asked when he was close.

"Yeah. What the hell is it?"

"I think it's him."

"Our guy? The fuckin' pied piper?"

"Yeah."

Hicks raised his rifle and peered through the optics. "You want me to go kill 'im?"

He whispered it casually, as if offering a drink of water. The certainty in his voice, the utter confidence he could do it, sent a shiver up Ethan's spine.

"No. Not yet," he said. "If we kill him here, we still have the horde to contend with. We need to get to Steel City first. We can't handle all these ghouls by ourselves. We need help."

"So let us follow him," Holland said. "Me and Hicks. We'll keep eyes on him. You and Cole get to Steel City and warn the people there. We can radio updates as we go."

Ethan nodded. "Good thinking. Just be careful, you hear? Stay out of sight. Do not, I repeat, *do not* fucking engage. Just keep me updated on his position. I'll radio back with a plan once we reach Steel City."

Holland was skeptical. "You really think they're gonna help?"

"I can't be sure, but Zeb seems convinced. He's been right so far, so that's what we're going with."

"No worries bossman," Hicks said, checking his rifle and switching out the batteries in his NVGs. "We'll keep you in the loop. Just do the same for us. Fair enough?"

"Fair enough."

The woodsman and the sharpshooter split up and headed out after the horde. Hicks turned north while Holland swung around to the south. In less than twenty yards, they melted into the foliage and Ethan lost sight of them. *Glad those two are on our side.*

He turned to find the others staring at him.

"You sure about this?" Zeb asked, jerking his head toward the horde. "Seems like your men are taking a hell of a risk."

"They'll be fine," Ethan replied. "We're soldiers. This is what we do."

EIGHTEEN

Now that I knew his name—even though he had no idea I was rattling around in here—Gideon seemed determined to frustrate and enrage me.

After the destruction of the town by the river, he led the horde along all through the night. During that time, it occurred to me I had never seen him sleep. Not once. He was clearly on drugs, probably meth, and must have had enough supplies to stay amped up continuously. But even the most determined fiend needs to rest now and then, so he led us off the main road and ran ahead at top speed. Noises rang through the woods, loud to our sensitive ears, and when we reached them, we were trapped.

Gideon led us to a shallow gully, the end of which he'd blocked with heavy branches and a few deadfall trees. I watched him skirt around the barrier, scramble up a tree, and climb into a makeshift hammock. By simply dangling there like a meat piñata, he kept the attention of the swarm and ensured none of us would try to leave. The barrier in front of us stopped our forward motion—less through structural integrity than sheer cussed messiness—and the few ghouls to make any progress became hopelessly tangled in the thing, making it that much harder for the rest of us to move forward.

Clever bastard.

My body tried to reach him, along with the rest of the swarm, and for a while the two of us were in harmony, my anger shining inside my head like a star. It wasn't just the terrible things Gideon had done that ignited my hatred, it was his disdain for the gift of life. Real life, not the shadow of it I was trapped in. Here he was, a survivor at the end of the world, and still he kills. Still he destroys. The notion fed my rage for the next few hours as he slept above the forest floor.

My body had a seemingly endless supply of energy and a bottomless capacity for hunger, but I didn't. Eventually I ran out of juice and gave into emotional exhaustion. I felt better after a while, which is stupid. But that's how the mind works, you know? You weep, and rage, and when it's all done, you have a rush of chemicals to boost you up. That--

Wait a minute.

I felt better. That meant my body was still doing something for my mind. There had to be some kind of connection between us, however thin and weak.

Gideon rose and sauntered away from the swarm, leaving us trapped in the blocked-off little gully. My anger rose up again and without thinking about it, I reached for him. My right arm lifted to point in the direction of his dwindling outline.

Holy shit.

Excitement raced through me like a flash flood in a parched canyon. With the desperation of the truly hopeless, I tried everything I could think of. I tried to move my hand again, my legs, turn my head, shift my eyes. I forgot about Gideon completely as I ran through the mental checklist of Things I Used To Do All The Time.

I got nothing. Nada. Whatever connected me to my body's functions, it wasn't something I could turn on and off like a switch. I took stock, no longer giddy about the possibilities but not despondent, either. I let my body work away on autopilot for a time and went over it every second, again and again.

After an hour or two, I came to a conclusion: It was the burst of anger that did it. My mind hummed with the desire to hurt Gideon, and my body's vicious hunger felt it. Responded to it.

For a few seconds, I laughed like a madman in my own skull. First out of victory for finding a way to interact with the world, and then because a funny thought struck me. Funny, and sort of disturbing.

Was this how crazy people felt? Was my body disturbed by the laughing, crying, screaming voice inside of it? *I was that voice*. The thought led me down a rabbit hole of possibilities, and my internal guffaws cut short when I came to the next logical question:

Was I insane?

It made sense, after all. A world destroyed by reanimated dead people? That's the stuff of bad movies. What if everything I had done, all the people my body killed, were just victims in the sane world seen through the filter of my own madness?

The thought chilled me. I wrestled with it for a long while but eventually decided I was sane. Crazy people rarely question themselves, and the world didn't seem distorted or weird. Aside from the circumstances around me, everything was logical. There were no giant unicorns or magical beings. Just a lot of death and destruction and sadness.

Only a few minutes after deciding Gideon was a real threat and not just a figment of my diseased mind, he came back. Judging by the grin on his wasted face, I made the right call.

Across his back was another rocket launcher, the tube strapped in an X with his rifle. He stood at the back of the gully, clapping his hands and urging the swarm to turn in his direction. It took a long time, but eventually the horde cleared the rise and followed Gideon down the trail.

It was slow going. Slower, in fact, than it needed to be. Several times, the madman led us off in a different direction, forgoing the use of his gun only to check the position of the sun and lead us back near the main road. We followed the path of a drunken giant, weaving off the road and back on dozens of times. Some of the detours were only a matter of hundreds of feet, others more than half a mile.

In the early afternoon, I found myself on the edge of the swarm, far off to the right. We were on another one of our wobbly detours, angling toward a set of railroad tracks in the distance. Gideon wasn't far ahead of the foremost ghoul, perhaps thirty feet. He was banging a pair of sticks together lightly to keep our attention, his eyes locked forward and his body twitching in anticipation of whatever horror he planned to commit.

My body heard a noise, the creak of leather and a faint jingling, too silent for living ears but perfectly audible to my body's enhanced hearing. My neck creaked to the right, giving me a long glance at the railroad tracks up the hill about two-hundred yards away.

There were men there, small as mice in the distance. My body tried to react, turning toward them, but Gideon's steady beat drew its attention immediately. I let a surge of anger flow between us to reinforce the reaction, and once my body was focused again on the evil bastard ahead of us, I did the mental equivalent of sitting back in an armchair to think.

My look at the men had only lasted a few seconds. We were already drifting back toward the main road, away from the railroad tracks, so chances were slim I'd see any of them again. Several men on horseback, but the hooves silent. Must have muffled them somehow. A few others on foot, dressed in combat fatigues, and none of them looked like pushovers.

I didn't know what lay ahead of the swarm. There could be big thriving cities full of dangerous people armed to the teeth. But from what I'd seen of the world, and what I could remember of my old life, I doubted it. The men following the tracks hadn't seemed aimless. It made sense to assume they were heading in the same direction as the swarm.

As the light fell, I knew the days ahead might be bloody.

*****

Swarms of dead people don't move very fast, and I got bored.

Rather than slip into a mental stupor and let the time speed by, I practiced focusing my anger and moving my limbs. For hours, from failing light to risen moon, I tried to make my body do things. It was hit and miss at best, once leading to a stumbling fall. Gideon didn't notice, not that I think he'd have cared either way.

My body stood on its own and began to walk again. Slowly I honed the mental needle to a deadly point. It wasn't great shakes; the best I could manage was crude motions. Nothing graceful or subtle. Change of direction, raising a hand, turning my head, sure. Nine times out of ten. But no small finger gestures, no picking up speed or slowing down our walk. But it was progress. It gave me hope.

The night wore on and grew darker, but my spirits held firm. The predator I lived in moved into hunter mode, senses sharp and ready for the chase, but I didn't despair. Because the last thing I saw before Gideon caught my attention was those men noticing the swarm.

They saw us, and two of them slipped silently into the forest, following.

If they managed to get ahead of us, things could become very interesting, very fast. So I kept on practicing my control, gaining proficiency bit by bit. It might amount to nothing at all, but if a chance to get my hands on Gideon presented itself, I didn't want to miss it.

NINETEEN

They made good time the rest of the way Steel City, arriving shortly before nightfall.

Hicks and Holland soon established a visual on the murderer, to whom they gave the radio designation Ragman. Cole, meanwhile, got a second wind allowing them to set a faster pace. The tracks eventually crossed a cracked stretch of two-lane highway, which they followed all the way to the fortress's gates. When they were within sight of the main entrance Zeb and his men dismounted, leading their horses on foot.

Ethan quickly surmised where Steel City had gotten its name: The outer wall, comprised entirely of steel shipping containers stacked three high, formed a rough circle that squatted grimly in the midst of a massive concrete lot. Battlements of welded steel plates ringed the top of the wall, varying in height from three to six feet, dotted frequently with firing slits. Men and women armed with a variety of weapons patrolled the perimeter, keeping vigilant watch over goings on both inside and outside the wall.

Glancing around as they approached, Ethan guessed the concrete lot Steel City occupied must have spanned nearly an entire square mile. The town itself only covered about a third of the lot, while neatly arranged shipping containers—enough to double the town's outer wall—occupied another large corner. On the northeast section, the flattened remains of an enormous warehouse distribution center lay slowly crumbling, surrounded by the burned out husks of dozens of tractor-trailers. Looking at it, Ethan remembered a story his friend Steve McCray had told him, and suddenly made a connection.

Six months after the Outbreak—about three months after Ethan joined the Army—a group of insurgents led by a militant, pseudo-Christian lunatic set up shop in a massive warehouse and declared themselves a sovereign nation. The Sons of New

Zion, or some such idiocy. Once established, they had set about burning, looting, and pillaging everything in sight, not to mention harassing military forces in the region.

It wasn't long before Fort Bragg and Pope AFB got their shit together, killed off the majority of infected surrounding them, and started mounting reclamation efforts. To that end, they made dealing with the Sons of New Zion their first order of business. A team of Special Forces operators led by Lieutenant McCray, who was subsequently promoted to captain, located the warehouse, reconnoitered it for a few days, and then watched from a good safe distance while a pair of F-16s dropped JDAM missiles on the insurgents' heads.

Problem solved.

And now, it seemed, the Sons of New Zion compound had been replaced by Steel City. From what Zeb had told them on the way in, the people living here had a reputation for decency and fairness, so long as visitors to their community followed the rules. Steel City was a place of trade and commerce, and the town's leadership had enacted a set of fair, but strictly enforced laws. These laws prohibited slavery, thievery, violence, and most forms of vice, including prostitution. Alcohol and marijuana were tolerated, but drunkenness and disorderly conduct were not. Other than that, as long as you minded your own business, conducted your trades in good faith, and didn't start any trouble, life in Steel City was good. But step out of line, and you were likely to learn what a week in the stocks or the business end of a cat-o'-nine-tails felt like.

As they drew close, Ethan saw the large main gate was partially open to allow carts and wagons through, as well as a smaller door for foot traffic. A contingent of guards stopped everyone seeking entry, looked them over, and checked their cargo for contraband. Anyone showing signs of illness was turned away. Everyone else was allowed to proceed inside. Ethan noticed that the guards, and the people who seemed to be permanent residents, all wore metal pins on their outer garments with the letters SC etched in black on a painted red background.

"What's with the pins?" Ethan asked, stepping closer to Zeb.

"Identifies the town's citizens. Takes a long time to earn one. You have to get at least three citizens in good standing to vouch for you, and then you have to be sworn in by the governor. The sheriff and anyone on the city council can veto a citizenship application, but they have to give a reason for doing so. A majority vote of the city council can override a veto, but that's never happened."

"Why not?"

"Folks around here are willin' to live and let live, but they ain't very trusting. Like I said, it takes a long time to earn your citizenship around here. If you do, it ain't likely anybody's gonna object to you joining up."

Cole spoke up from behind them, "What's stopping someone from just making a fake pin and blending in?"

Zeb chuckled. "Son, I would strongly recommend against trying that. There's only a few hundred citizens here, and they all know each other by name. If any one of them spotted an unfamiliar face with a citizenship pin, well…let's just say they don't take kindly to that sort of thing."

The big gunner nodded. "Duly noted."

"All right now fellas," Zeb said, pushing back the brim of his hat. "Y'all stay quiet and follow my lead." He handed his horse's reins to Hedges and set off toward the gate. Michael's mouth flattened into a thin line as he watched his uncle walk away, one hand drifting toward the pistol under his coat.

There was a line of people waiting to get in, laden with heavy packs and carts full of trade items, but Zeb ignored them and walked straight up to the guards at the pedestrian entrance. A chorus of shouting and complaints went up in his wake.

"Hey you, stop right there!" the guard closest to the doorway shouted, drawing a pistol. Zeb held up his hands.

"Come on now, Dale. Don't tell me it's been so long you don't recognize me."

The guard lowered his weapon and squinted. "Sheriff Austin? That you?"

Zeb smiled. "The one and only."

The guard holstered his weapon and motioned him forward. "Just you," he said. "Your men have to wait."

Zeb turned. "You mind, fellas?"

"Not at all," Ethan replied, "We'll be right here."

Zeb exchanged a few low sentences with Dale and two of the other guards. After a few moments, he stabbed a finger behind him and made a series of impassioned gestures. The guards' faces went pale. Dale leaned over and whispered something to one of them, who turned on his heel and sprinted through the gate. A few more words went back and forth before Zeb shook hands with the remaining guards and returned to brief the others.

"I told 'em what's happening, the short version anyway. They're rounding up an escort to take us straight to the governor's office."

"You must have some serious pull around here," Cole remarked. "Looks like these people trust you."

"Fort Unity does a lot of business with this place, and I don't just mean bartering. When marauders, or big hordes, or whatever else shows up, we send troops to help each other out. Sort of an alliance, you see."

Ethan nodded. "Which is why you think they'll help us with the swarm."

"Exactly."

Cole pointed over Zeb's shoulder. "Looks like we're about to find out."

Six men approached them, all armed to the teeth, and at their head was a stocky, middle-aged man of medium height with a bald head, broad shoulders, and a pair of hard, intelligent green eyes. He stopped in front of Ethan and Cole, subjected them to a brief, intense scrutiny, then turned to address Zeb.

"I appreciate you coming to warn us, Sheriff Austin."

"It's the least I could do. This is Staff Sergeant Ethan Thompson, and this is Sergeant Isaac Cole, both out of Fort Bragg. I ran into them back near Hamlet and told them about the trouble we've been having. They agreed to help me investigate Broken Bridge. I'm sure you remember Chris and Mike."

Davis shook hands and exchanged a quick greeting with them, then turned his attention back to the soldiers. "I'm Rory Davis, sheriff of Steel City."

Ethan spoke up, "Pleased to meet you sir."

"Are you here on behalf of yourself, or the Army?"

"Both, actually. I volunteered for this mission, but I still take orders from Central Command."

Davis gazed at him for a long moment, his expression giving nothing away. "The governor will need to speak with you. I'll escort you to her office."

He turned and walked back toward the gate while his men spread out on either side of Ethan and Cole. Zeb noticed the soldiers' tension at being surrounded.

"Take it easy fellas, they don't mean any harm. There's a lot of folks around here with ill feelings towards the military. This is for your protection."

"I'm sure it is," Ethan said, although he wasn't sure at all. Cole shot him a glare and shook his head, but didn't argue.

Sheriff Davis' men were impassive as they led the soldiers through the gate.

*****

The first thing Ethan saw was the secondary wall.

Constructed much the same as the first one, it was simply another ring of cargo containers—only one unit high this time—about thirty feet from the outer ring. Machine gun nests, sniper stations, and guard towers populated the top of the inner perimeter, which also boasted welded steel bulwarks for defenders to take cover behind. There was another gate, smaller than the one outside, but this one had been opened wide to allow access to the main gate. It was through here that Davis' men led Ethan, and as they passed, he noticed that the sides of the containers bulged out a bit, as though under pressure from something inside them.

"Dirt," Zeb said, noticing where Ethan was looking. "They're all full of dirt. And rocks, and bricks, and concrete blocks, and anything else that might slow down a bullet. The containers themselves ain't bulletproof, you know."

That had occurred to Ethan, but he hadn't bothered mentioning it. "Looks like a pretty solid place. Easy to defend, tough to attack. They've got some salvaged military hardware as well." He pointed at a fifty-caliber machine gun mounted in a tower above them.

"That a problem, Sergeant?"

"Not at all. If anything, the Army will trade them ammo for food. We've got plenty of ordnance, it's chow we're always short on."

"Hm. You might want to mention that to the governor when you talk to her."

"I might do that."

The buildings, homes, and businesses were, much like the outer wall, made of shipping containers. Most of them were single units with windows and doorways cut out of the sides, but some were more creatively constructed. To Ethan's left, he saw two containers stacked on top of each other with a third intersecting them in an L shape. The two containers on ground level held shelves and display stands stocked with vegetables, fish, live chickens, eggs, and still-bleeding cuts of wild hog, among which over a dozen people had gathered to peruse the goods and haggle with a pair of harried-looking clerks. The container stacked above the grocery stalls appeared to be living quarters, as evidenced by clothes hanging from lines on the roof and a pair of crudely wired solar panels next to a large antenna.

As they moved deeper into Steel City, Ethan realized the town was laid out in a series of concentric circles except for the wide, triangular market plaza near the main gate. The smells and noise of the market faded behind him, transitioning into a calmer, more peaceful residential section. The container-houses were numerous enough to form streets and alleys, and Ethan quickly became lost as Davis' men led him through a winding set of twists and turns.

Finally, they arrived at a wooden building, which stood out like a sore thumb amidst the sea of metal surrounding it, where they were ordered to halt and surrender their weapons. They handed them over nervously, then followed Davis and his men inside. The building was small, only a little larger than a house, with a large, open lobby ringed by desks behind which city employees scribbled diligently and shuffled papers. Staircases ran up both of the far walls, leading to a line of offices on the upper floor fronted by a narrow balcony. As Ethan and the others entered, the people behind the desks—old women, for the most part—barely spared them a glance.

Ethan noticed they kept only one hand on their desks, with the other below the tabletop, out of sight. He also noticed the desks were arranged such that if the clerks were to start shooting, they were out of each other's line of fire. *Never underestimate old women with guns.*

Davis motioned for everyone to follow him up the stairs, and just as Ethan's foot was about to hit the first step, his radio crackled in his ear.

"Echo Lead, Echo One. How copy?" Hicks' voice was pitched low, almost a whisper.

Ethan stopped and held up a hand. "Hang on just a second. I'm getting a call from my scouts." He keyed the mike. "Copy loud and clear, Echo One. What's your sitrep? Over."

"We're about four miles or so south of Steel City. I think the Ragman's plannin' to stop for a little while. He led his horde off the road and stopped 'em under a cliff on the sheer side of a hill."

"What's he doing?"

"Right now, nothin'. He's up on top of the cliff just sittin' and starin'. Sumbitch looks about half dead hisself."

"Copy. Keep eyes on him, but stay out of sight. Keep me updated. Over."

"Will do, boss. Echo One out."

Davis raised an eyebrow. "News?"

"My scouts are following the man responsible for what happened in Broken Bridge. He seems to have stopped for the moment."

"Good. The governor needs to hear this. Let's go."

He led them to a door near the center of the walkway and knocked gently. A female voice spoke from inside. "Come on in Sheriff."

Davis opened the door and motioned to Ethan and Zeb. "Just you two. The rest of you wait here."

Cole and Ethan exchanged a short glance. The big gunner gave his squad leader a slight nod, then stepped back and leaned against the wall, arms crossed over his chest.

"Don't worry. I ain't going nowhere."

By his expression and his tone, Cole made it clear he was being polite for the moment. But if he heard anything in the governor's office he didn't like, things were going to get ugly. The guards detected the big man's hostility, and backed off just a bit, hands close to their weapons. Michael and Hedges read the situation, and decided to go wait in the lobby.

Ethan and Zeb stepped into the office, followed by Davis and two of his men. The door shut behind them, and a plump little old woman with a cloud of curly gray hair and thick bifocals perched on her nose stood up from behind a modest desk.

"Sheriff Austin, what a wonderful surprise!" She stepped around the desk and approached Zeb with her arms out. The old lawman smiled and gave her a warm hug.

"Good to see you too, Margaret."

She stepped back and turned to Ethan, one hand outstretched. "And who's our new friend here?"

Ethan shook her hand and smiled. "Staff Sergeant Ethan Thompson, First Reconnaissance Expeditionary."

"Ah, the famous First Recon, also known as The Wreckers. Your unit's reputation precedes you."

Is that a good thing or a bad thing? "Thank you, ma'am."

"Call me Margaret. Or Governor Warren, if you want to be formal about it. I don't care much either way. Zebulon gets to call me Margie, but that's only because he's so darned handsome."

She swatted Zeb on the arm, shuffled back behind her desk with a chuckle, and motioned Ethan and Zeb toward a pair of chairs. As they sat down, Ethan was acutely aware of the presence of Sheriff Davis and his men standing behind him. Taking a breath, he forced himself to relax.

"Now Zeb, as nice as it is to see you again, I'm going to go ahead and say you're not here on a social call." She crossed her hands in front of her and leaned forward.

"I'm afraid not."

He gave her the rundown of what happened to Broken Bridge, the other towns that had gone dark, and Ethan's men finding and following the man responsible. By the time he was done, Governor Warren's shoulders slumped and her watery blue eyes glistened with unshed tears. She stayed silent for a few long minutes, staring into nowhere. Finally, she seemed to gather herself, cleared her throat, and sat up straight.

"What happened to our neighbors is a tragedy, Zeb. One we cannot allow to go unpunished."

"I couldn't agree more."

She shifted her gaze to Ethan. The pleasant light that had been in her eyes earlier was gone, replaced by simmering anger and a shrewd, calculating intelligence. Ethan began to understand why the hardened people of Steel City looked to this diminutive, motherly old woman for leadership. "So your men are watching this Ragman as we speak, correct?"

He nodded. "That's right ma'am."

"And your scout thinks he's preparing to stop?"

"Yes ma'am."

She rubbed her chin thoughtfully. "Well, that gives us options. We could just have your men kill the son of a bitch, but that still leaves the question of the horde. If it's as big as you say it is, then it most likely comprises a significant portion of the infected in our area. If we can destroy them all, it'll go a long way toward making life safer for this town and the people we trade with."

"We could wait until he falls asleep," Davis said. "If he corrals the horde, it'll make it easy to destroy them. Sergeant Thompson could have his scouts apprehend the suspect and bring him back to stand trial. Then my people could move in and deal with the infected."

The governor glanced up skeptically. She reminded Ethan of a schoolteacher addressing an unruly child. "Sheriff, have you ever fought a horde that large before?"

It was a long instant before he answered. "No ma'am."

"So how can you be sure your people could handle it without taking casualties, especially considering it will be dark outside in less than an hour?"

Another pause. "There's no way to be sure, but my people know the risks, ma'am. They'll do whatever it takes to protect this town."

“I’m sure they would, Sheriff. I’m not calling into question their courage or their capabilities. Nor yours for that matter. But I don’t like dealing with unknowns when it’s possible to stack the odds in my favor. Furthermore, I don’t like my constituents risking their lives unnecessarily.”

Davis struggled for something to say for a few seconds, but then Zeb spoke up. “You look like you got a plan rattling around in that head o’ yours, Margie. What’re you thinking?”

She shifted her attention, letting Davis off the hook. “Well, let’s first look at what we can verify. We know, or at least strongly suspect, that this murderer used a LAW rocket to destroy the gate at Broken Bridge, correct?” She tilted her head toward Ethan.

“I can’t say with a hundred-percent certainty, but I’m pretty sure.”

“Right. And judging by the path he’s taking, it’s a safe bet he’s headed our way. If he is, and if he has access to more such weapons, he’ll most certainly use them against us in much the same manner as he did Broken Bridge. Furthermore, as we speak, this Ragman is less than five miles from our gates. The only reasonable conclusion we can draw from this is that he plans to rest before launching his assault on our town. We could simply launch a pre-emptive attack, but that leaves too many variables on the table. I don’t like variables.”

She stood up and walked toward a table in the far corner of the room. On top of it was a hand-drawn map depicting Steel City and the surrounding area. She motioned for everyone to join her, and when they had gathered around, she pointed at a series of interconnecting straight lines that represented the inner and outer wall.

“A LAW rocket is a powerful weapon, but judging by the damage it did in Broken Bridge, it’s nothing we couldn’t repair in a day’s time. That’s one of the many benefits of building our defenses with shipping containers: they’re modular. We can move them wherever we need to. We can set up a decoy at the main gate, let him in with his horde, and close the trap behind them once they're inside. The inner wall will act as containment. But all of this will be predicated upon the Ragman believing that once he's through the outer gate, the inner gate won't be much of a defense. So we'll wait until nightfall, and then very quietly switch out the inner gate with a few loaded containers. Shouldn't take more than a few minutes."

"Really?" Ethan asked, surprised. "I mean, shipping containers are pretty heavy even when they're empty. The ones at the wall are full of dirt and stuff, right? How do you move them?"

The governor smiled. "Forklifts."

"Forklifts?"

"Yes, Sergeant. Forklifts. Propane powered ones. We have quite a few at our disposal, as well as an adequate supply of fuel. Very handy machines."

Should have thought of that. This used to be a distribution center, after all. "Right. Got it."

"Here's what we'll do," Governor Warren continued, "Sergeant Thompson, I'll need you to stay in contact with your men and keep us all appraised of what the Ragman is doing, as well as the position of his horde. If I had to bet on it, I'd say he's going to rest for a while, then leave the horde at some point to case the town's defenses, assuming he hasn't done so already. If your men can stay on his trail and report his activities to us, we'll be able to prepare accordingly."

"We can do that."

"Very good. Sheriff Davis, I want you to carry on business as usual, but spread the word among your deputies about what's going on. Quietly, if you please. We don't want to start a panic."

"Yes ma'am," he said.

"Zebulon, our town's hospitality is open to you, as always. Feel free to make yourself at home. You and your men can take a room at the guard barracks if you like. If it's not too much trouble, though, I may need to deputize you gentlemen when the time comes to prepare for the attack. Crowd control and such. Would you be willing to help with that?"

"Of course, Margie. Whatever you need."

"All right then. Sergeant Thompson, you can use the office next door to coordinate your efforts. There's fresh water there, and a washbowl. I can have some food brought up if you need it."

"I'd appreciate that. To be honest, I could use a bite to eat."

"I'll see to it then." She turned and faced the room, determination set on her small, wrinkly face.

"We have work to do, gentlemen. Let's get it done."

*****

As it turned out, the little government building had electricity.

Ethan hadn't seen them walking in, but the entire south-facing side of the roof was covered in solar panels. When he mentioned to Governor Warren that the batteries on his communications equipment were beginning to run low, she directed him to a recharging station on the first floor. He connected his handset, updated his location and mission log on the ruggedized tablet, and then powered up the wideband transmitter.

His first order of business was to radio FOB Harkin. The usual indifferent private was gone this time, replaced by a much more businesslike sergeant. In just a few minutes, Colonel Lanning came on the line.

"Good to hear from you, Echo Lead. I was beginning to worry."

"We're doing fine, sir. I'm in Steel City as we speak."

"Any luck finding that horde?"

"Yes sir. Not only did we locate it, we got ahead of it, and I've got two scouts monitoring its movement as we speak."

"Out-fucking-standing. Did your scouts find the piece of shit leading 'em around?"

"Affirmative. They have him under surveillance as well."

"Surveillance? Why isn't he dead, or at least apprehended?"

Ethan related Governor Warren's plan to trap both the Ragman and his horde by using the walls of Steel City as a cage. After he finished, Lanning was silent for a few seconds.

"That's a hell of a dangerous plan. Does the governor know what a LAW can do?"

"Yes sir, she's aware," Ethan replied. "She says she's willing to risk it, and she says her people can fix the damage in a few hours. I'm not crazy about the idea, but I have to admit she has a point. The more infected we kill, the safer life will be going forward for the people living here."

"What about collateral damage? How's she going to keep her own people from getting killed?"

"That I'm not so sure of. The local sheriff is spreading the word among his men about what's going on. I think they plan to lock the place down at nightfall and move everyone into the inner perimeter. It's what I would do, anyway."

"Either way, it's on her if things go pear-shaped. What does she have you doing?"

"For now, I'm staying in touch with the scouts and keeping Warren in the loop. If I can, I'll try to coordinate things once the horde arrives, which will probably be sometime tomorrow after dark. I've got the best comms gear in town, and I don't think the governor will have a problem with letting the Army handle the dangerous stuff."

"I imagine not. Is there anything I can do from my end?"

"Actually, there is. Do you have access to any night vision equipment?"

"I had a feeling you were going to ask for that. You have any idea how hard it is to requisition that stuff?"

"Yes sir, I do. But we're talking about hundreds of civilian lives here. All I need is a couple of night vision scopes."

Lanning sighed. "I think I can handle that. What about the infected, though? If this bat-shit crazy plan works, how are you going to kill them all?"

"*I'm* not doing shit. That part is up to the governor. But if you could spare some guys from the 82nd to help out, it would go a long way toward repairing these people's opinions of the military. Know what I mean?"

"Understood. I'll look into it. Keep your radio handy, Sergeant. I want regular updates. I'll have someone contact you once your supply drop is inbound."

"I appreciate that sir. Not just the drop, but all your help."

"That's what we're here for, Staff Sergeant. Talk to you soon."

"Copy. Echo Lead out."

TWENTY

Gideon gnawed on stale beef jerky as he led the swarm onward.

He didn't want the food, didn't even feel like it was a necessity, but the last dregs of self-awareness in him knew his body needed fuel. It would be nightfall soon, and for the first time in twelve hours of constant movement, Gideon questioned the need to move so far off the path.

At first, it seemed logical. The road was a heavily traveled route for traders and merchants, after all. Even the end of the world wasn't enough to drive a stake through the heart of American capitalism. But after traveling for miles without spotting a single person, he began to wonder if he was on the right path. Had Gideon sobered up long enough to consider the situation clearly, he would have realized the road he walked on ran straight from Broken Bridge. The chances of anyone coming from there were slim to none.

Then again, had he been thinking clearly, he wouldn't have been killing people.

Steel City was close. Already, he could almost smell the blood, iron in his nostrils and copper on his tongue. He never *tried* to taste the blood, but there was always so much splattering around. Some always got in his mouth. After a while, he started to like it.

His desire to see the arrogant survivors brought low bordered on a need. There was no room left in him for pity or remorse, no hunger inside but to see bright futures snuffed out. If random chance could do it, why not him?

Another brief moment of lucidity tried to happen, but Gideon snorted a pile of powdered Meth from one dirty fingernail and cut that shit off fast. The muted flash of pleasure did nothing to obscure the facts: He'd wasted most of a day with his meandering path toward Steel City. The swarm was close—

dangerously so—and could hit the place in short order. The only problem was the sun shining overhead. The attack had to be at night, as were the others. Daylight gave the enemy the ability to see and move unhindered. Night created confusion, fear, and bred mistakes.

Below the kinetic rush of twitching muscles and tremors in his hands, Gideon was tired. A deeper man might consider it emotional exhaustion as well as physical, a mind tired of the death and destruction. But he wasn't that man. Nothing close to it.

With the swarm close behind, Gideon drifted into a nearby stretch of woods. He spotted a craggy wall where a section of forest floor dropped away from the side of a hill. Twenty feet up, a ledge jutted out. He checked to make sure the majority of the swarm was still with him, then pushed up a sleeve and slashed lightly at his forearm.

Blood welled up, a scarlet almost black against his mealy skin. Gideon wasted no time scaling the weathered stone, fingers slipping into cracks with manic surety. Thirty seconds later, he sat on the ledge, feet dangling as he watched the swarm.

Dead faces gave him their undivided attention. The hungry, vacant stares were like a thousand mirrors converging on him. As much as he hated people for their freedom to live, Gideon still found room in his heart to hate these things as well. Making them his weapon was a small victory, but he took no comfort in it. Watching them pine for his blood as the scent of it wafted down the cliff brought a sneer of contempt to his wasted face.

The sea of bodies below him wavered like prairie grass. He rolled onto his side, faced toward them, and tucked his legs onto the shelf. The motion of the crowd was hypnotic, making him drowsy as he watched. Something was off about it though. Some part of the pattern didn't match up. Just as he slid off into disturbed and fruitless slumber, it hit him.

One of them is standing still.

*****

I watched Gideon sleep, which is actually creepier than it sounds since I'm a dead person. He fell off fast, like a soldier or prisoner would, no warning at all. I'd done my best to get close to him as the night transformed into day. I knew as soon as he showed up with another tank-busting weapon things were going to get bad.

Crazy people with rocket launchers. The math isn't hard.

I wanted to get closer, but the swarm had swollen to the point where even moving among them was nearly impossible. After Gideon climbed his perch and nodded off, I redoubled my efforts to connect with my body. If I wanted to get close to the bastard, I'd need more than the ability to point or turn my head. I already had some gross control over direction, but it needed refinement.

So I started by standing still. It was a lot harder than it sounds.

Living people manage their balance without much thought. The constant flex of muscles and tendons are motions so small we usually don't notice them. Dead people do the same, but with less control. It's messy and awkward, exaggerated and visible.

Bearing down on the endless sway of my body as we stood there, I let the rage out in a controlled release while concentrating on being motionless. To my great surprise, it worked. More than that, I could feel my feet and legs. My mind tapped into my nervous system, making it possible to balance while standing still almost as if my body knew what was needed.

After a little while, the effort grew tiring. I held it for as long as I could, finally releasing my hold and taking a breather. There was a certain feeling when I had control, a strange sensation like the rush you get when finally figuring out a tough math problem. After a short rest, I searched for that state of mind again, letting the anger build up and flow out.

There. *There*.

I moved forward. Not just my body, but both of us. The steps were halting at first, buffeted on all sides by the writhing dead. I moved with increasing confidence, even managing to brush a ghoul out of my way as I walked. Such a simple thing to a living person, but so amazing to me.

I stood at the edge of the stone face, the scent of Gideon's blood wrapping around me like a warm blanket. It invaded my senses, the smell so powerful it transitioned into taste. The heady aroma sent waves of hunger through my body. It wanted the blood with a savage power that sent shivers into the reptile part of my brain.

Which was fine. I wanted it too, if for different reasons.

Night turned to day, and the sun was high overhead when Gideon woke. By that point, I had walked the crowd several times. I watched him stretch, and groan, and strap on his weapons. I watched him fill his body with poison and grin madly as he scampered down. He tossed a fresh dash of blood down the cliff, then disappeared around the side of the hill and stayed gone until the sun was low in the sky, barely an angry red lump peering over the horizon. The horde remained where it was, locked in place by the scent of his blood. When he finally came back, he looked happier than ever.

"Come on you pieces of shit," he said, smiling and clacking his sticks together. "It's showtime!" The horde obeyed, and I was swept along with them.

Dusk wasn't far off, which meant whatever was going down was happening soon.

*****

Like the grand marshal of the world's worst parade, Gideon marched in front. Less than a mile from the gates, he felt the glorious rush of victory, premature but within his reach.

Steel City was an honest name. The place was built on a trucking depot of some kind, the sort of place lost in a sea of steel shipping containers of every color and shape. Someone had the brilliant idea to build a wall with them, a huge triple-layered circle wide enough to house hundreds.

Casing the place was easy. He just hid in a distant tree on a tall hill and sighted down the scope of his rifle. The front gate was huge and thick, perhaps too much for his stolen arsenal to handle. The possibility would have bothered him but for the smaller, thinner door cut into the heavier gate. He had watched the larger gate close but the smaller one stay open to accommodate foot traffic. Merchants and traders called on the place right up until dark, when the gates were all shut and sealed.

But even closed, that thin, man-sized gate would pose no problem for his rocket.

Once through the main gate, breaching the inner gate behind it would be easy. The bailey between the outer and inner walls was meant to be a killing floor, but the second gate wasn't meant to stop swarms. During his first observation, the inner gate hadn't been closed at all. A fast enough assault with the element of surprise might net him a straight walk in, his thousand hungry soldiers at his back.

As he approached the town with his horde, the darkening sky was overcast, blocking even the feeble light of the moon. There were only two lookouts, both perched atop the stacked container walls, lazing in lawn chairs. Gideon saw their outlines against the dark gray nighttime clouds as he approached ahead of the swarm. In his dark coat and clothes, ragged hair down around his face, he was all but invisible.

Two hundred yards. One fifty, then a hundred. The lounging guards didn't so much as stir.

Gideon slowed from a sprint to a jog, coming within fifty yards. With a practiced motion, he pulled the rifle around on its strap. Without thought, without hesitance, and utterly without remorse, he raised the weapon and sighted through its scope.

One shot, center mass, then a pivot to the second for a repeat performance. Two cracks rang out into the night, the sharp slap of sound waves beckoning to the swarm behind. Gideon adjusted his sights, checked the targets again, and chuckled wetly. The angle was better than he thought; neither lookout had moved an inch. Now he had to move quickly; if more guards came, he'd have to stop and shoot them too. The monster inside him purred at the thought, which made him smile.

If it liked that little show, it was going to love what came next.

*****

A thousand bodies followed Gideon as he moved toward the target, but I was closest. Constant practice had brought me to a marionette level of control, jerky but mostly functional. It took everything I had and I felt the waves of mental exhaustion building up behind the stone wall of my will, but I was committed.

I was starting to feel alive again. By that I mean the normal sensations of having a body of my own were returning, not just the sensory data. I didn't feel like a helpless passenger any more. My body was beginning to respond on instinct. Little things, but as I stoked the fires of my emotions to maintain control, I felt that same harmony eating away at me. My body reacted to me, took in part of me, but I was experiencing the same. The hunger gnawed at my belly, not at all revolting. The primal urge to tear Gideon apart made my fingers twitch, and bound together with my own desire, it was a force nearly too powerful to control.

Almost.

While it was difficult, the sense of joining with my body was also empowering. Movement came more naturally, I felt stronger, and I was even gaining on Gideon as he slowed down from a full run to a full stop. I stalked closer as I watched him fire his rifle. My enhanced hearing picked up the dark laughter following the kills.

Well ... what I thought were kills, anyway.

The noxious scent of burned cordite should have been followed with the rich tang of fresh blood. I couldn't see the victims, but Gideon's reaction could only mean the guards above were dead.

Yet as I approached, I smelled nothing.

The monster ahead of me looked through his sights once more, unaware that the monster behind him moved faster than his brethren. I was fifty feet away, then thirty, then fifteen. Nearly close enough to leap on him, were I capable of it. Close enough to catch every vagrant smell polluting the air around his body. The stink of his unwashed flesh mixed with old death and the rot inside him, probably from the drugs.

Then he moved, hopping to his feet and darting forward another fifty or sixty feet. This time he stopped but stayed standing, reached behind his back, and shouldered the rocket launcher. The sense of glee from my body mirrored itself in my brain as I drew closer.

I would get him this time, no question.

Logic stepped in and turned the knob on my self-preservation instinct up to eleven. A brief struggle for control followed, my weary brain wrestling with my own desires and those of my walking corpse. If we kept moving forward, we would likely catch on fire from the belching gas and flames soon to bathe the area behind Gideon.

In my panicked haste, I defaulted to logic, screaming inside my own head about the danger. My body couldn't have given less of a shit about that. It wanted what I wanted, and didn't understand my frantic sense of alarm.

So I yanked the valve off my fear and blasted the emotion out as loudly as I could, raw and unfiltered. That, combined with the simple direction to go left, *now*, was just enough to make it happen. As Gideon settled the weapon in place and aimed, I swerved a few feet to one side and stopped. The rest of the swarm would be on us soon, chewing up the yards even now.

Fire, dammit. Before they get here. You're mine, *motherfucker.*

TWENTY-ONE

Darkness had fallen over Steel City.

For several hours the night before, Hicks and Holland had maintained surveillance. When it became clear the Ragman wasn't going anywhere, Ethan called them back to town. A few hours' sleep and a quick meal later, they left again, worried the Ragman might have moved on.

He didn't.

He lay right where they last saw him, sound asleep.

Around noon, Hicks called in that the Ragman was awake and headed toward Steel City, but had left the horde behind. A couple of hours later, he was less than half a mile away studying the town from a hilltop. Davis and the guards carried on business as usual until they finally got word that the Ragman was going back to retrieve the horde. That was when they put the governor's plan into motion.

All visitors were turned away with a warning that a horde was inbound. Those with too heavy a load to flee were permitted inside, but kept under watch. The guards closed the main gate, then had a small team of forklift operators move the secondary gate out of the way and replace it with two well-loaded shipping containers. A few more containers were positioned outside the main gate to seal the trap once the horde was in, but the operators didn't have night vision equipment, so Ethan called Hicks back to coordinate with them. After that, it was a waiting game.

Where the guards normally patrolled on the main gate, Davis had put two mannequins dressed to look like his guards in lawn chairs. It wasn't the best strategy to fool the Ragman—the ruse wouldn't have worked for a second during the day—but under cover of darkness, the madman might not notice the difference. If he did, Ethan was the insurance policy.

For long hours, he sat still in his sniper hide on the outer gate, hidden behind a battlement. Through his night vision scope—dropped off via helicopter thanks to Colonel Lanning—Ethan watched the forest at the edge of the concrete lot. Just after midnight, he spotted movement.

Waving, staggering forms flowed through the forest like a flood in slow motion. At their head, just as he'd hoped, was the man he was looking for.

The Ragman.

In his crosshairs.

"All stations, Echo Lead. I have visual on the Ragman. Repeat, visual on the Ragman. All stations stand by."

Which is to say, nobody fucking move. In fits and starts, the scrawny, wasted figure approached the main gate while stopping frequently to let the horde catch up before setting off again. Ethan began to hear a few faint, distant moans as the ghouls drew closer. Behind the murderer, he saw a tall, gaunt-looking ghoul in shredded clothes drawing ahead of the horde. It lurched along far faster than the average walker, and seemed to move with greater purpose. Through the scope, he saw its unblinking eyes locked on the back of the Ragman, hands extended, fingers curled into claws. *That's weird.*

Finally, the Ragman sprinted ahead, faster this time, and stopped to unsling a canister from his back. *LAW. Just like I thought.* Ethan watched him fumble with it in the dark for just a moment, and then raise it to his shoulder. There had been a time when he'd thought the designers of such weapons to be geniuses for making them so easy to use, but now he was realizing that rockets didn't care who they killed. And when they fell into the wrong hands, they were the stuff of nightmares.

He ducked deeper behind cover and keyed his radio. "Brace for impact!"

First came the *crack,* high and piercing, almost like a firecracker but infinitely louder. Less than a second later came a terrific *BOOM,* deep and powerful. The shock of it traveled through nearly eighty yards of steel and thumped upward into Ethan's stomach, rendering him breathless and causing a hollow pounding in his chest.

Fuck me.

He sucked in a deep, painful breath and leveled his scope again. The Ragman had already run through the gate, his gaunt face shining with glee, smiling through broken teeth. The horde swarmed in behind him, filling up the narrow hole where the secondary gate used to be and cutting off his escape. He sprinted a few feet further, no doubt nearly blind in the darkness, and stopped short just before hitting the inner wall. His face transitioned from unbridled joy, to confusion, and finally, to panic. Behind him, one of the ghouls—the same tall, fast one from before—was nearly on top of him.

Ethan grinned. *Gotcha motherfucker.*

"All stations, Echo Lead. Ragman is in the cage. Repeat, Ragman is in the cage. Perimeter team, hold position and stand by. I want to trap as many of these ghouls as we can. Acknowledge."

Hicks' voice spoke in his ear. "Copy, Echo Lead. Perimeter team standing by."

Ethan sat up, positioned his rifle comfortably on the battlement, and settled in to watch the show.

*****

Gideon stared at the place where the flimsy inner gate should have been.

Not only flimsy, but *open.* Instead of an easy entry with an army of the dead at his back, before him lay a wall of unforgiving steel. The dust and flickering embers around him from the rocket's explosion were details so minor they were non-events. The gate was gone. That was the only fact that mattered.

Time slowed to a crawl. He tried to wrap his addled brain around the reality before him. He'd seen it, sure enough. Watched men and women move through it. There was no question the gate had existed, but now?

Nothing.

The dim, suppressed part of his brain responsible for rational behavior clamored for his attention, but Gideon paid it no mind. The shock of finding his easy path into Steel City not blocked but *gone*, vanished as if it had never been, was just too much.

His slack-jawed stare couldn't have lasted more than a few seconds, but they felt like an eternity. Cold realization hit his veins in a wave of ice water. Things weren't going his way. This was bad. Really bad. Gideon looked around for someone to blame, head swiveling on rusty hinges, but of course, there was only him.

Then something grabbed his back, and Gideon screamed.

Fear invaded him for the first time in ages as the strap across his chest pulled tight and he leapt forward. *The gun*. His attacker had the rifle. He writhed as he moved away, twisting his torso down to slither out of the rifle's strap. His hand darted to his belt, flashing silver on the return trip, and in less than three seconds, Gideon was free of his attacker, armed with a blade, and facing the enemy.

It was one of his ghouls. The thing stood there staring at him, which by itself was unnerving as hell. It held the rifle in one wasted hand, fingers gnarled tight around the barrel just above the forestock. Behind the ghoul, the rest of the dead moved on ungainly legs toward them. The sight of his own army in front of him rather than at his back sent Gideon into a rage. The blame fell on this fucking thing in front of him, the idiotic corpse holding his gun. Just a lucky snatch at an easy meal by one dead man out of a thousand.

Whatever bonds held the monster in check fell away. Gideon felt the last strained threads of his sanity fray and break.

He stabbed at the dead man. The first thrust caught the rifle, almost as if the dead man moved to intercept. The gun clattered to the pavement as he jammed the knife forward again, a scream of rage spraying flecks of spittle across the dead man's face.

The second time was the charm. Gideon felt the knife slide home, point gouging through flesh and bone, the grind of steel muffled and wet.

In his excitement, he'd forgotten the most important rule—maybe the *only* important rule—in dealing with the infected.

Always go for the head.

The ghoul's eyes locked on his as the thing wrenched its hand away. Gideon lost his grip on the weapon, which pierced the dead man's hand all the way to the hilt.

He was running before the creature could grab at him again.

*****

Gideon ran from me, but rather than the frustration of losing him again, I felt the thrill of the hunt. He'd stopped as soon as he stepped through the smoldering remains of the front gate as if dumbfounded by what he saw.

Our little tussle had left him weaponless, as far as I knew, and terrified. Grabbing for the rifle gave me a sense of victory that came with a full-body high, but smelling the trail of fear-soaked sweat he left behind topped it.

I wanted to be disturbed by that. Really.

Knife jutting through my hand, I summoned my rage and pushed as hard as I could to follow. The narrow lane between stacks of containers was devoid of people. I heard and smelled the cluster of dead men and women working their way through the shattered gate behind me. There wouldn't be much time; they'd catch Gideon's scent easily.

My body moved in a rolling, awkward run. It wouldn't win any gold medals, but for outpacing the rest of the shambling corpses behind me, it worked. The dank odor of the man grew stronger as I worked my way around the broad curves of the killing floor. The wide circle defined by the path in front of me suddenly stopped. Another shipping container sat astride the way forward, creating a dead end. Gideon had his back to the wrinkled steel wall of the thing, hands spread wide and breathing hard. It wasn't the first good look I'd had at the man, but it was certainly my last. Whatever else happened, the dead moving behind me were a sure bet he wouldn't walk out of here alive.

He turned to face me, whites showing all around his wide pupils, filthy hair plastered to a forehead streaked with clean places in the grime where sweat poured down. I savored the moment. Every strained line of his face was a moment of joy. The crazed tension in his body a spring waiting for the catch to be released.

This was a man who knew he was going to die, and that his dying would be hard.

I approached him at a walk, tasting every fresh breath of terror wafting between us. Away from the majority of the swarm, Gideon's panicked breathing was all I could hear until I got a little closer. My body's attuned senses picked up a sound so low a normal human wouldn't have heard it. Nothing major, just a thin scrape of fabric against metal, weirdly amplified by the steel walls around me.

I knew the direction, of course. I looked toward the man watching us from above and saw him peering at me through the scope of a rifle. Throwing caution to the wind and hoping like hell he wouldn’t pull the trigger, I raised a hand to him in a short wave. The hand in question had six inches of steel jammed through it, but it was the best I could do. Gideon's head jerked to the side, looking for whatever I'd seen, desperate hope written on his face.

Seizing the opportunity, I lunged forward.

His throat parted like a rare steak, salty blood coursing down my face. The ragged beard ripped away as I gnashed again and again, and when the burbling scream rose from his chest, the wind of it blew from a gaping hole in his neck and into my mouth.

All control vanished. I didn't need it anymore, didn't want it. I'd wandered aimlessly for days—weeks—with no hope of ever being more than I was, just a man trapped in a body.

Now, a murderer was dying between my teeth, and I felt a dark satisfaction. I couldn't remember my own name, nor that of my child. My wife was a treasure that kept me going, but as I surrendered to the urges pouring in from my body, I knew it was not enough. Old memories aren't what keeps us going even in the best of times. It's making new ones, truly living, that pushes us forward. I was beyond that. The admission came hard, even if only to myself.

So I gave in. I let go. My mind relaxed like a clenched fist slowly expanding. I felt my body begin to invade, tearing away at the edges of every emotion, and thought, and memory that had made me who I was. The man I had once been. I let it all burn, consumed by the festering infection that had taken my life away. Better oblivion than this constant fight.

Gideon died beneath me, but my body kept on. For an unknown time, I fed. Gideon struggled, then went limp. Others joined me. When the hunger abated, I summoned the last vestiges of my humanity and stood up. I turned back toward the man hiding above me with the big scope on his rifle. I raised my hand again, imploringly this time. He shifted and brought his rifle to bear.

The last thing I heard was a muffled crack.

And then darkness.

TWENTY-TWO

The sound of gunfire echoed long into the morning.

Just after dawn, two Chinooks arrived with forty troops from the 82nd Airborne and a crate of ammunition. When they touched down, Ethan met with the lieutenant in charge and briefed him on the situation. Ten minutes later, the lieutenant had his men form neat ranks on the inner and outer wall, and gave the order to open fire. While they worked, the governor and Sheriff Davis organized a work detail of over a hundred people to begin excavating the mass graves where they planned to dispose of the bodies. The forklifts would make moving them from one place to another easy, but the digging still had to be done by hand. Watching them work, Ethan wondered how big of a hole it would take to bury over a thousand corpses. He wasn't sure he wanted to know.

Cole, Hicks, and Holland gathered on the wall near the main gate where they had a good view of the extermination. They took no satisfaction from watching the ghouls die; it was just something that needed doing. Tedious and grotesque, but necessary. Normally they would have participated, but after forty-eight hours with nearly zero sleep and very little food, they were ready for a break.

Following a brief meeting with the governor—who made a show of expressing her sincere gratitude to the Army as loudly as she could to the throngs of people standing nearby—Ethan said his goodbyes and joined his troops on the wall. Zeb and his men made their rounds and then followed soon after.

"I appreciate all your help, gentlemen," the old sheriff said, shaking each soldier's hand in turn. "Don't know if we could have pulled this off without you. I know we got off to a bad start, but I'm damn glad we ran into you fellas."

"Likewise," Ethan replied. "I'm just glad we stopped that crazy bastard before anyone else got killed."

The smile faded from Zeb's face. "Yeah. I just wish we'd stopped him sooner, you know?"

Ethan nodded. "We did the best we could Zeb. We saved this town, and there are a lot of people alive today who wouldn't be if not for us. Don't forget that."

Zeb stared at his boots while Hedges and Michael said their goodbyes. When they were finished, he tipped his hat to Ethan and led his men back down the ladder. A few minutes later, they rode their horses through the gate and turned north, back toward Fort Unity. To the east, the sun rose higher in the sky and cast their shadows long across the pale brown grass.

"So now what?" Holland asked as he watched the lawmen ride away.

"Now we go retrieve our gear," Ethan said. "Head over to the governor's office and radio FOB Harkin for pickup. The helo should be able to put us down near where we left our packs. After that, we'll see about catching up with the U-trac."

"Fan-fucking-tastic." Holland turned and began climbing down the ladder. "I can't tell you how excited I am about riding that goddamn thing again. Eating shitty food, barely sleeping, sucking down jet fumes, getting shot at. I'm getting a hard-on just thinking about it."

Hicks chuckled quietly and shouldered his rifle. "Reckon I better go with him. Make sure he stays out of trouble."

"I'd appreciate that," Ethan replied.

The gunshots kept up a steady cadence as the troops from the 82nd went about their business. Cole and Ethan stood side by side and watched them while they waited for Holland and Hicks to return. At the main gate, a team of workers had already removed the section of wall damaged by the LAW rocket and were busy welding a new pedestrian entrance out of steel plates. True to the governor's word, they would have the gate fixed in just a few hours.

Ethan's expression grew troubled as his mind wandered back to the previous night's events. He'd tried to put it out of his mind, but now that things had quieted down, the memories were breaking loose from their cages. Over and over again, he saw the last seconds of the Ragman's life and the strange ghoul that killed him. Ethan didn't doubt his sanity or his eyesight, but he was having a hard time coming to grips with what he'd witnessed, and what it might mean. Everything he knew about the walking dead had just been turned on its head, and he wasn't sure what to do about it.

"Something wrong?" Cole asked, noticing his squad leader's distraction.

Ethan opened his mouth, hesitated, closed it, and then tried again. "It's just…I saw something weird last night. You're gonna think I'm crazy."

"What happened?"

"I was over there by that battlement when the horde came in. The guy leading them, the Ragman, he was right below me when the ghouls got him."

"Okay. So why is that weird?"

"The one that killed him…it uh…I think it might have waved at me."

Ethan turned to look at Cole, expecting some kind of joke or his friend's usual boisterous laughter. Instead, the big man's expression was somber. "Tell me what you saw."

"Well, the Ragman was right below me, like I said, and the ghoul that got him was way ahead of the others. It moved faster than I've ever seen one of them go. The damn thing was almost running. When it got close, I shifted my aim to take it out, and I think it heard me. It looked right at me, Isaac. I swear on my mother's grave, it looked right at me and it raised its hand like this." Ethan waved a hand in the air, demonstrating. "Like it *wanted* me to see it. The Ragman looked where it was waving, and then *bam*, the ghoul was on him."

Ethan drew his jacket tighter around him, jamming his hands in his pockets. It was a cold morning, but the chill he felt had nothing to do with the weather. "After it killed him, when the other ghouls showed up, it stood up. That was the weirdest thing, I've never seen one of them do that. You know how they get, right? They get a hold of food, and they're like fucking rats—you can't pry 'em off with a crowbar. But not this one. It stood up, it looked right at me, and it waved again. I know you think I'm yanking your chain, Isaac, but I swear to God, that's what happened. I wouldn't believe it myself if I hadn't seen it with my own eyes."

Cole's expression hadn't changed. "What did you do then?"

He shrugged. "I shot it. Thing is though, I think that's what it wanted. I think it *wanted* me to shoot it."

Cole was silent for a long time after that, his eyes distant. When he finally spoke, it was slow and hesitant. "I don't think you're crazy, Ethan, and I don't think you would lie to me about something like that. But that's pretty goddamn strange."

Ethan shuffled his feet. "What do you think it means?"

"I don't know, man." Cole shook his head. "I don't know."

The two soldiers watched quietly for a while as the detachment from the 82nd wiped out the last of the horde. When their work was done, they piled into the Chinooks and took flight back toward FOB Harkin, but left their crate of ammo sitting in the market square. Ethan had a feeling it wasn't an accident.

He and Cole climbed down from the wall and were silent as they walked through the main gate. Hicks and Holland joined them a short time later, and they shared a quick meal of MREs while waiting for the helicopter. No one spoke as they ate, all of them lost in their own thoughts. An hour later, a Blackhawk touched down in a field nearby, and after letting Ethan and his men retrieve their packs, the pilot turned the chopper due west on an intercept course with the U-trac and the rest of First Platoon.

As the ground sped by below, alternating between forest canopy, overgrown fields, and abandoned towns, Ethan thought about Broken Bridge. He thought about those poor murdered people, all dead because of one madman's desire to kill. It was unfathomable to Ethan what could drive a person to do such horrible things. To burn and destroy for the sake of burning and destroying. And the worst part about it, the thing that frightened him the most, was it had just been *one* man. Just one. What if there had been more, working together? He shivered at the thought.

The Blackhawk passed over Charlotte on its way to the Tennessee border. Below it, a million walking corpses craned their necks to watch it pass, their undead eyes locked to it as it traced through the sky. It continued westward, growing smaller and smaller on the horizon.

Eventually, it disappeared.

About the Authors:

James N. Cook (who prefers to be called Jim, even though his wife insists on calling him James) is a martial arts enthusiast, a veteran of the U.S. Navy, a former cubicle dweller, and the author of the "Surviving the Dead" series. He hikes, he goes camping, he travels a lot, and he has trouble staying in one spot for very long. Even though he is a grown man, he enjoys video games, graphic novels, and gratuitous violence. He lives in North Carolina (for now) with his wife, son, two vicious attack dogs, and a cat that is scarcely aware of his existence.

Joshua Guess (who prefers to be called Josh but uses Joshua because his mother freaking *demands* he use it professionally) is a jack of many trades. He has training in martial arts, survival, fire/rescue, emergency medicine, and a host of other areas. Between intense bouts of writing, he enjoys movie nights with his wife, good meals at local diners, and trying to catch a nap without one of his cats using him as a pillow. Residing in Frankfort, Kentucky, he spends most days cooped up in his office with a giant dog, dim lighting, and too many ideas to keep in his head.

If you enjoyed The Passenger, you may also like the exciting zombie apocalypse thriller *Victim Zero*, by Joshua Guess. Read on for a preview!

Chapter One

Kelvin McDonald, who was only called by his rightful first name when some woman or another in his family was angry, sat in his office long after his staff went home for the day. It had been seven years since that last trip before being awarded his doctorates; seven years of constant research into the strange organism he'd drunkenly dubbed Chimera on a night out with his team members.

The world hadn't really been a different place then, but looking back on how much of his life changed from that day, it seemed like someone else had lived it. He had entered college at sixteen, sought after by every university with a science program to speak of. Full scholarships offered and finally accepted, Kell found a home at Stanford. He remembered those first few days on campus; a tall and gangly black kid, too young to need a shave more than every third day, southern accent not thick enough to get him laughed at but always present and commented on by the west-coast cast of characters around him.

His first few days were hard, but in the biology department he fit in for the first time. The memory of discussing microbiological theory and favorite research papers with peers sharing his excitement was a treasured one. Like an heirloom, Kell took that one out often. It was polished and beautiful and sharply detailed. His first few days at Stanford were a major turning point in his life.

At twenty-six he went on that trip, ten years of hard work that would have been twelve or thirteen if not for his brilliant mind and perfect recall. Before his next birthday he was awarded those sheepskins; one specialized in microbiology, the other in genetics. Kell had always suspected the initial months he'd dedicated to studying Chimera had played a part in the decision to grant his doctorates. It wasn't a secret the faculty wanted him on staff as a researcher. Indeed, it worked out that way.

A year later Stanford was made an offer it couldn't refuse. Kell didn't know how much money exchanged hands, but the biotech company that bought out every scrap of Stanford's research into Chimera, Sinclair, was international and enormous. A few years before they'd been hit with a lawsuit decision that required a hundred-million dollar payout, and the company hadn't hesitated.

The only catch to the deal was that Kell came with it. The man who lived and breathed Chimera would have to leave his home of more than a decade.

Kell agreed with the proviso that if he were so vital to the company that they wouldn't buy the research without him attached, he got to choose where he did his work.

The office he sat in, with only the recess lights burning, was the place he'd settled after leaving the university. An hour and a half north of his home, the Cincinnati division of Sinclair Global was his. Entirely his—no other work went on in the subdued building.

The phone on his desk rang, and Kell answered.

"Kelvin McDonald," he said.

"Doctor McDonald," the voice on the other end replied. "This is Jim Mitchell. You were told to wait for my call?"

Of course I was, you idiot. Why else would I be here an hour late?

"Yes, sir," Kell said.

"Good, Good," Mitchell said. "Let me tell you what this is all about, then. You've been working on Chimera variants that repair nerve damage, correct?"

Kell inhaled sharply. "Yes, that's right, but--"

Mitchell cut him off. "And how would you categorize the success of those variants, Dr. McDonald?"

“I'd call them good, so far,” Kell said. “But in need of a lot of work.” He made an effort to keep his voice even, calm. Mitchell was a vice-president.

“Is that so?” Mitchell asked. “I think you're being modest, Doctor. You've been testing the variants on primates for months now, haven't you? With a total success rate?”

Kell fought the urge to grind his teeth. “Yes, but there are concerns. Chimera is extremely difficult to control. It evolves within a subject. In lower order test subjects, there were always mutations that created unexpected results.”

“But not undesired results?”

Kell snorted. “You're pushing for something, Mr. Mitchell. I won't sit here and explain the complexities of Chimera. You want to tell or ask me something, and you want to hear that I'm confident about where our research stands. Why?”

Mitchell paused for a moment. “I think you are confident, Doctor. I also think you're being overly cautious. Aside from one incident last year, my understanding is the Chimera organism has given overwhelmingly positive results. I want to know your opinion on moving to human trials.”

Kell didn't hesitate. “It's an incredibly bad idea. Not only will we not be eligible for clearance on that for several years, but Chimera seems to be more active in more complex life forms. As you pointed out, last year we lost sixty-seven mice in less than an hour. That was due to a mutation, and all those animals died from a single test subject being introduced to the population. I'm sure you read the report, sir, but if I feel my position is more grounded in reality it's only because I was cleaning out the shredded corpses of more than four dozen mice. I saw that with my own eyes, touched it with my hands.”

Mitchell cleared his throat. “So you're telling me you are absolutely opposed to human trials?”

Kell felt relief wash over him. “Yes, sir. I am. Even if we could get clearance, this organism is simply too dangerous and our understanding too limited. I've been working with it for seven years and even I have barely scratched the surface. As quickly as Chimera evolved in that single mouse, it did so four times as fast in our primates. In humans the generational changes would be at least as quick and not necessarily for the better."

There was a long silence. Kell began to think Mitchell had ended the call, but caught the faint sound of the other man breathing.

"That's very unfortunate, Doctor McDonald. Because Sinclair Global received a special dispensation for human trials three months ago, and half a billion dollars in DARPA backing to escalate our research."

Kell swore. Loudly.

Mitchell chuckled nervously. "Understandable reaction, but you're going to like this next part even less. Tomorrow you'll be receiving a visit from some workers who will be installing a basic isolation unit in an unused section of your lab. You see, Dr. McDonald, we've had our Boston lab working with the primate variants for six months, and the first human subject began trials three weeks ago. There have been...complications. And we need your expertise."

Kell's free hand gripped the edge of his desk so hard he felt the heavy wood creak. "How long until this patient arrives, if I may ask?" Kell said with icy formality.

"Oh, he'll be there in about six hours, actually. We're sending him in a temporary unit housed within a shipping container. Transitional staff will stay with him until you arrive at work tomorrow morning. Then he's all yours."

Kell pinched the bridge of his nose and for the first time in his life wished he'd gone into mathematics or physics or wizardry. Something harmless.

"Yes, sir," Kell said. "I'll be here."

*****

Karen was already in the shower and baby Jennifer in her crib, when Kell finally made it home. Kell thought about slipping behind the curtain to join his wife but reconsidered when he remembered her habit of keeping a loaded .38 on the towel rack next to the tub. One break-in was enough to teach her caution.

Instead he stood over his newborn daughter and watched her sleep for a while. She fidgeted, tiny hands grasping and flexing as she did the baby equivalent of chasing rabbits. Strange how a person only eight weeks old could change everything about a person. Kell became interested in biology from sheer wonder as a child. Some people looked to the sky in awe at all the things that vastness contained, but he was always fascinated by the mysteries found in the smallest parts of living creatures.

Every cell a puzzle, every strand of DNA a conundrum waiting to be tinkered with and explored.

Yet here before him lay an enigma even he couldn't wrap his mind around. He and his wife made love, and then followed the meiotic dance that created an entirely new human being. It was so simple, so basic, yet that one primal act of creation moved forward with time to make his daughter. She would be her own person in the end, a collection of small mysteries of her own.

Feather-gentle, he ran a finger over her fine hair.

"She's been sleeping for an hour," Karen said from behind him.

The tendon in Kell's jaw twitched, his only sign of surprise. Five years together had given his wife a good working knowledge of his reactions. It was a game of hers, to constantly try to get more than an involuntary twinge from him. Karen sometimes called him 'Buddha' for his unshakable calm.

If only she could have seen him a few hours before.

She put a hand to the back of his neck, using him as a fulcrum to pull herself high enough to kiss his cheek. He trembled as she did it, the stress of the day finally becoming too much.

Karen put a hand on his shoulder lightly and turned him to face her. She wasn't short, but even at five foot eight she had to crane her neck to look him in the eyes. Hers were hazel flecked with gold, a striking match to her deep tan skin. Her mother was from South Africa, her father American but ethnically Indian. Both of them were lawyers, and their beautiful daughter, she of the almond-shaped eyes and wavy black hair, had followed in their footsteps.

"What's wrong?"

Kell considered the question much longer than absolutely necessary. It wasn't that he didn't trust his wife—she was a lawyer, after all, and knew how to keep confidence—but she also knew about non-disclosure agreements, of which he was under at least half a dozen. Beyond that, the work he did was cutting-edge and frankly dangerous to know about.

So, he compromised.

Kell sat on the edge of the bed. "I can't tell you the details, honey. But basically I've been put in a position where I had to choose between letting someone else deal with a complicated problem they might screw up, and taking it on myself."

Karen nodded as she sat next to him in her fluffy red bathrobe. "I assume that this has to do with your research?"

Kell nodded. "Of course. Sinclair has always wanted me for only one reason."

She put a hand on his leg. "You've always been able to trust your staff with tough problems. What makes this one different?"

"This time there could be...larger implications. You know I've always been strongly against creating potential weapons or pathogens. That's not what I'm dealing with, but a screwup could be just as bad. Maybe worse."

Her fingers tightened on his leg. "And you think you're the right man to fix it?"

Kell nodded again.

Karen gave his leg a slap. "You're damn right you are. No one has been working on this as long as you. Your own professors handed Chimera over to you when they couldn't figure it out. You're not just the right man for the job, baby. You might be the only man for it. If safety and diligence is important here, I can't think of anyone on the planet better suited to the task."

Kell smiled at her, but it was weak. Which led her to slap him on the back of the head. It was gentle. Mostly. Then she pointed a finger in his face, and he knew she was getting serious.

"Look, Kell. Just because I've been on maternity leave and not carrying around a metric ton of stress doesn't mean I'm gonna let you get away with self-pity. You might be in a tough spot, but you didn't make it. You got handed a mess; you know you're the one who should clean it up. Not because you made it, but because anyone else runs the risk of just screwing it up worse."

She leaned over and kissed his shoulder. "So stop moping about it. That's not going to do you any good. Sleep on it, deal with it, then move forward. It's not like you have any choice."

"I know, Karen, I just worry that...ah, Jesus it's hard to even explain without telling you everything."

She rolled her eyes. "I don't need details to know you shouldn't be worrying yourself to death over something you have to do and can't change. Maybe me saying that won't make it better, but I promised your momma I'd set you straight for the rest of your natural life. You knew that when you signed the papers, and look; you managed to live with that decision just fine."

Kell couldn't help laughing. He snaked an arm around her waist and pulled her close. Her lips tasted like raspberries—her favorite lip gloss. She must have put it on as soon as she hopped out of the shower. Though he'd fallen for her hard many years before, it was small gestures that kept him falling in love in little ways every single day. It got him through the lonely nights when she was stuck at the office. It kept his hand steady and mind sharp when dealing with potentially dangerous organisms with a penchant for unpredictable mutations.

"You're right, of course," Kell said, running a hand over his shaved head. "I'll get on with it. I'll probably bitch about it for days, but you're used to that by now. And let's face it, you aren't going to divorce me over that. You only do what Mom tells you because she makes you dinner twice a week. You won't give that up."

She poked a finger into his slight paunch. "Well, one of us could suffer without for a while."

Laughing, he slid his own hand under her robe and across the damp skin of her belly.

"Maybe I could do with a little exercise instead," he said.

To Read on, pick up a copy of *Victim Zero* on Amazon today!

Made in the USA
Lexington, KY
07 November 2015